Subdivision

Subdivision

Stories by
STEPHEN AMIDON

THE ECCO PRESS

Copyright © 1991 by Stephen Amidon
All rights reserved

First published by The Ecco Press in 1992
100 West Broad Street, Hopewell, NJ 08525
Published simultaneously in Canada by
Penguin Books Canada Ltd., Ontario
Printed in the United States of America
This edition by arrangement with Bloomsbury Publishers, Ltd.

Library of Congress Cataloging-in-Publication Data

Amidon, Stephen.
  Subdivision / Stephen Amidon.
    p.   cm.
    $18.95
    I. Title.
PR6051.M47S8   1992   823'.914—dc20   91-37853 CIP
  ISBN 0-88001-279-X (cloth)

CONTENTS

Subdivision

Scatter

Rene waited for the drugged spasms of muscles, insane rushes at the bars, screeches like shattering glass – anything to break the silence and interrupt the regular beating of her heart. But they remained perfectly still, a blankness in their eyes. Even those without straps seemed frozen in the lab's sterile light. Not sleeping, not poised and watchful. Just still, breathing with measured sighs, as if nothing more were possible.

'Why don't they move?'

'They aren't supposed to. They're conditioned to respond only to the pain the doctors give them,' Paul answered, not looking.

'But what if they have an itch or something?'

'They don't.'

Paul worked here part time. His father, the business manager of the laboratory, had created the job to keep his son busy between school and dinner. His benefits included the minimum wage and a key, which he sometimes used after hours. This was the first time he had brought Rene. When she asked him what it was exactly he did, he simply

I

said that he was a 'handler'. She pressed him for details but he said nothing else.

'Here.'

She took the joint from him. The first hit was all paper, so she let it go and took another. She watched the smoke turn blue against the stainless steel and fluorescent light.

'Can't we turn off some of these lights?'

'No. There isn't a switch. They stay on all the time.'

She watched the thinning cloud of smoke drift between the bars of the cages above them. The monkeys ignored it resolutely. With their dead eyes and wire skull caps, they looked to her like weary monks. She felt an urge to yell something at them, make hideous faces and rattle the padlocks. But she remembered what Paul had said. She'd have to hurt them. So she let them be, envying their distance from everything.

The drug crowded into her mind, chasing away her thoughts. A vague warmth welled in her throat, her breasts and fingertips. She looked down at Paul, lying on the tile floor. He was taking small, studious hits from the joint, looking at nothing. Or perhaps everything. His eyes were so large and prominent that he seemed to be without blind spots, to miss nothing around him. His pupils would remain perfectly still for long intervals, then refocus so rapidly that Rene could not detect the motion. Paul was like that – long, absolute stillnesses, punctuated by rapid and graceful movements.

'Hey,' she said.

He made to hand her the joint, but she gestured it away. He took another quick hit, then stood and walked to the nearest cage. It contained a rhesus monkey, bound to the back wall by a leather strap around the waist. Its left arm was taped flush against its torso, an atrophied hand hanging beneath loops of thick gauze. Its free arm had been broken in two places, so that it stuck out to the side in a slight gesture of supplication. A tube carrying clear liquid was taped into a corner of its mouth.

'Think he'd like a hit?' Paul asked, holding the joint up to the bars. The animal's soft eyes focused on the orange tip. Rene laughed and told him don't. Paul flipped the joint into a large sink with several hook-shaped faucets. It hissed for an instant.

'What do they eat?'

'Different things. Depends. Vegetables, sometimes. Usually just nutritional fluids. Those ones over there are being starved to death.'

'Why?'

Paul shrugged.

'Do they have names?'

'No.'

'Are they killed when they're through with them?'

'Most. It's part of the process. Some are recycled.'

He was looking into the cages now.

'Hey,' she said.

Paul walked across the laboratory, knelt in front of Rene and kissed her. His mouth tasted good, sweet smoke and flesh. He unbuttoned her blouse and touched her breasts, running his hands over them until his thumb and fingers came together on each nipple. He squeezed too hard at first, but relaxed when she twisted slightly away. He used to hurt her in a hundred small ways, but now hardly ever. She finished taking off her blouse, then removed his shirt. She liked his chest, the vertical line of hair, the muscles. He put his weight on her, laying her back. She was surprised to find the tile floor was not cold. They pulled awkwardly at each other's jeans for a moment, then tended to their own. She had to undulate her hips, knees, then feet to work them off. He simply backed off her and was naked in an instant. She didn't like lying in all the light, didn't like the hard floor against the base of her spine, but he was quickly in her and she stopped thinking. He slid into her without foreplay or guidance, pushing hard and fast. She turned her head reflexively, pressing her cheekbone into the humming tile. She laid a hand against his face, felt the deep furrows in his forehead and his hard, dry lips. For a moment, he seemed to push everything through the top of her head, leaving a perfect vacuum.

He came quickly, but she was used to that. In fact, she preferred it this way – the absence of prelude, the short duration, the abrupt stop. Like a shock. If it lasted longer, it would begin to fill up her mind, control her. It would become an event, a thing: it would exist, have a name, require thought, recollection, anticipation. It would become something they did, in sequence with other things they did. Paul kept it as it should be – a piece of nothingness.

He sank a bit to one side of her, slowed his breathing. She ran her fingertips over the periodic crests of his spine, trying not to think, holding to the dullness in her mind. But soon she found herself wondering about the source of the humming in the floor. What time it was. What Paul was thinking. Why the lights had to be on all the time.

'I wonder what they think.'

Paul didn't answer. She squeezed him impatiently.

'Nothing.'

'Don't they ever fight back?'

He rolled completely off her. She thought he was annoyed, but he was only showing her his hands. He held them limply before her, palms down, emphasizing the series of small scars running from the knuckles to the wrist. She had noticed them before but hadn't asked.

'From them?'

'The new ones, sometimes. But the doctors can purge the fight from them pretty quick. You'd be surprised.'

She explored the scars with her fingertips.

'Why don't you turn them loose?'

He stood and began to sort the clothes.

'They'd starve. Or wander out onto the Beltway and get run over, trying to get at the headlights. They're conditioned to move to light in a field of darkness. It's a reflex they develop for testing.'

He snapped the elastic band of his underpants.

'Besides, I'd get fired.'

She dressed while he eliminated traces that they had been there. As they were leaving she noticed a row of deeper cages.

'Raccoons . . . '

These were all motion, pacing, pawing the air, moving their jaws obsessively. One was chewing on a bar with manic deliberation. Tagged, frothed, self-scarred, they seemed ready to attack anything. A faint fecal odor surrounded their cages, a cushion against the lab's sterility. Rene noticed how different their eyes seemed from the monkeys' – crazed, surprised, attentive.

'They're rabid,' Paul explained. 'Most of them are from the marshlands, but some were found in town. It's getting kind of out of hand. The doctors haven't been able to isolate this particular strain. It's pretty virulent.'

'Has anybody been bitten?'

Paul shrugged his shoulders.

Dave and Skip came by to get them in Skip's car, a dark green Mustang Skip had inherited from his older brother. Dave drove. He raced the car through the empty, unlit streets of Research Park, a sprawling colony of laboratories and scientific manufacturers located between the subdivision and the marshlands. A private security van with yellow lights gave them half-hearted chase for a few blocks, but broke off when it became evident that the Mustang was leaving the community. Skip suggested that they head out to the marshlands and do shots of vodka, but Dave had something else in mind. He turned up the radio as high as the speakers could take. He wasn't talking tonight, so nobody would. The DJ was deep into a set of Victor and the Vanquished. Pure hardcore – four chords a second and too many words to understand. She played the title song from 'Crib Death', then some cuts from their first album, 'Theater of Meat'. Rene followed the lyrics the best she could. The windows were closed tight against the fall chill, so before

5

long the sound had become a tight seal on their heads, letting nothing else in or out. The songs were so hard, so fast – just when she felt caught up in them they would stop, between chords, between words. Like somebody pulled a plug. She took the vodka bottle from Skip and drank. It stung for a moment and caused her throat to contract violently. But it quickly had an anesthetic effect upon her teeth and tongue.

Dave turned off Research Drive onto the business loop of Route 8, which served as the western boundary of the subdivision. To the east and north of the community was the Beltway, while the southern border consisted of Research Park. Further south still were the marshlands. They drove about a mile, past the high school and the street where Rene's parents lived. A picture of them flashed in her mind, her father sprawled shoeless on the couch, her mother a tableau of anxiety at the kitchen table. She drank again, chasing the images with the liquor.

Dave swung off the road into a supermarket parking lot, speeding past dumpsters, broken crates and rolls of wire. Then through an alley, past some corrugated sheds and a fenced area filled with empty drums, into another, recently paved parking lot. Several unfinished buildings crowded the unlined pavement, the largest of which was a three-story office complex destined to house attorneys, dentists and CPAs. Its façade consisted of a sparse metal frame and floor-to-ceiling plate-glass windows. The glass had obviously just been installed, for each window was crossed by bright strips of tape bearing the manufacturer's name and trademark. Dave stopped the car a few hundred feet from the building and cut the headlights. The only illumination in the area was a floodlamp attached to a mobile office on the opposite side of the lot, near the entrance to the alley.

'Come on,' Dave said to no one in particular.

He and Paul slid out of the car. Skip and Rene remained seated. Dave leaned back in.

'You not coming?'

6

Skip shook his head.

'Then give me those.'

Skip lifted a carton from the car floor and handed it to Dave. It contained forty-eight D-sized batteries they had taken from a truck. Dave cradled the carton beneath an arm and walked with Paul. They stopped twenty yards in front of the building. Dave squatted over the box, tearing at the tape and cardboard. As soon as he had it open, Paul grabbed a battery and, with a dancer's skip and full turn, hurled it through the center window of the top floor. The glass cracked into several large pieces, seemed to hover for an instant, then fell to the pavement. Before it had landed, Paul had sent another battery into the façade. Dave hustled to catch up and get in his fill. As they broke the rest of the glass, Skip told Rene his brother's story.

'Peter was a lot older than me, so much so that I figure one of us must've been a mistake. Anyway, he did poorly in high school because he was bored and didn't even go to college, which upset my parents until he got a job selling insecticides. He did pretty well and got promoted to Illinois, where he did really well. He was a good salesman to begin with, and the year he got out there there was this gypsy moth thing. So he made a bundle and got promoted again, so that he no longer had to be a salesman, just manage others. And he was only twenty-four. He married this older woman named Denise who I only met once and they bought a house. And then we heard that he was sick. Well, Dad went out there and when he came back he said Peter wasn't so much sick as in trouble. It seemed he was in this clinic to recover from alcoholism. Dad said Denise told him Peter would drink about a fifth of liquor every night, even more on weekends. The strange thing was, he was never hung over or sick at all. And he only drank at night, in his study. Never at lunch, not at bars or even when he traveled. Only at home. And he never broke anything or beat on Denise or the baby or even swore at them.'

7

Dave and Paul slid back into the car, breathing heavily. Dave drove them slowly back through the alley.

'Anyway, the people at the clinic said they'd fix him up, and Denise called a few weeks later and said that everything was all right. Peter was back home, totally dry, on Anabuse and mild barbs. Only that same night really late the phone rang again and it was this cop who said they'd had to shoot Peter because he had a knife to the baby's neck. After we buried him we got a letter from this doctor at the clinic explaining what'd happened. It seems that one part of Peter was a really good person and the other part was a madman. Schizo, you know. So the good part would drink like crazy whenever the bad part started to come out, which was whenever he was home. So the boozer and the nut canceled each other out and he just sat numb in his study, reading reports and old magazines. In limbo, is what the doctor said. But then they had the good part stop drinking and so there was nothing left to hold this bad part down and so the cops had to shoot it. Anyway, that's how I got this car.'

There was a block or so of silence.

'We broke them all, except for a couple on the top floor,' Dave said to no one in particular, and turned north onto the business loop.

Rene did not know Dave and Skip too well. Skip was not as short and skinny as he should have been, standing a little taller than Dave and outweighing Paul by a few pounds. Yet he had a certain withering demeanor that made him seem smaller than everyone, a certain transparency to his features that made him seem weaker. He had a sallow, edged face that betrayed too much intelligence, too many drugs. Dave was darker and sturdier, with blunt features and a thick body. He would have been handsome had it not been for a waxy scar running between his left nostril and temple. Someone had once bet him he couldn't flick a match into a gasoline can. His body always seemed to be flexing, as if trying to resolve an inner tension. His mouth worked incessantly, soundlessly, his teeth biting into his lips with unthinking brutality. Rene had noticed that when she spoke to him, he would never look at her eyes, but rather at her hands or waist or chin, as if anticipating some sudden attack. He gave her the feeling that he wasn't paying attention to what anyone said unless it happened to coincide with what he was thinking at the moment.

But she liked to drive around with them every once in a while. They would circle the Beltway or drive through the marshlands, getting wasted, listening to the radio and passing slower traffic. Occasionally, Dave would stop and they would tear something up. Mostly it was breaking glass, but recently they had also been setting dumpster fires. The first few attempts had been failures. Merely igniting surface paper didn't work – poor ventilation and the weight of the trash kept the fire from catching. So Paul had developed a method. They would hunt around for a tunnel – the cardboard tube rugs came wrapped around, some fiberglass plumbing – anything long and hollow. They would inject this into the center of the dumpster, then funnel in bits of smouldering cloth and paper. Next, Paul would balance atop the dumpster and blow steadily through the pipe until a good core of flame was established. It took a while, but once going, the fire would be nearly impossible to extinguish. They would watch for as long as it was safe. The dumpster eventually became a circus of burning, with the frantic exodus of slugs and mice, the blue-green flame of burning plastic and cellophane, the sporadic explosions of light bulbs and aerosol cans.

Dave and Paul usually did the work. Skip would join in only when they would 'futilize' something, as he called it, which consisted simply of depriving a machine of some essential part. Brute destruction held no charm for him, but knowing that somewhere there was a garbage truck without a carburetor or a phone booth minus a receiver sent him off for hours. Dave, too, seemed at times driven by some private logic in his choice of targets. It bothered Rene, the way he could seem so deliberate, as if he were following a script. It made it the same as everything else.

Mostly, she came to be with Paul. She liked the way he moved, quickly from one thing to another for no apparent reason. She liked the way he answered her questions – never explaining, never lying. Just answers. Most of the time he remained quiet, his eyes cast slightly down, some irony tugging at his upper lip. When they were wasted she would try to guess what he was thinking, but never asked him about it. She was constantly absorbing his silences, greedily feeding off his indifference. And when his silences would break out into violence, she would feel caught up out of events, out of her body, into nothingness. Sometimes she thought that while she was in his arms, he would turn one of those rapid movements against her, breaking her neck or strangling her. Through gesture and whispers she had tamed his caresses, but had not diminished this possibility, this presence which seemed so strong on these nights.

They had climbed down from the overpass, wedged themselves in the triangular cavity between the bridge and the concrete slope that led down to the Beltway. Skip was farthest in, giggling wildly at some forgotten joke. Then Dave, his twisted face half in shadow, dangling the vodka bottle in his hands. Paul was at the concrete's edge, propped on an elbow, facing Rene, who preferred to sit in the open on the grassless hill. Since it was a weeknight and late, traffic was light, mostly trucks passing below with heavy Dopplered hisses.

Dave let the bottle roll down the slope. It broke against the trestle with a short, loud noise. Skip laughed harder. There was a searchlight beating across the sky just to the west of them, advertising some all-night sale. Rene was following its course diligently when Paul broke the capsule under her nose. She had to blink hard for a moment as the acidic fumes penetrated her sinuses. She inhaled deeply, opened her eyes, and everything fell apart. The searchlight broke into fragments and turned loops overhead, a heavy chain holding them all down. The Beltway trucks became a wild stampede. Skip's laughter became the screams of a wounded animal. Then, dark liquid seemed to cover her eyes and something began to explode rhythmically in her head. It was as if with each instant, each percussion, she were given a different mind. She was a jagged shape of glass falling onto blacktop. She was in that limbo with Skip's brother. She was held to the backseat of a cage by leather straps. She was her mother doing coffee and cigarettes midmorning in the kitchen. She was lying beneath Paul in an empty room.

A few seconds later, all that remained was the searchlight and a slight headache. It occurred to her that the beating in her mind had been nothing more than echoes of the drugged racing of her heart.

'I want you guys to break up my house.'

'No,' said Dave. He was the judge of these things, dispenser of the complex and inexplicable set of rules governing their nights. The only reason behind them was that they were Dave's. Usually Skip made suggestions, on rare occasions Paul; Dave decided. They had come to know that breaking glass was good, breaking concrete or plaster was not. Killing animals was wrong, killing flowers was all right. These had become facts, as now was the 'no' which angered Rene. She had known what the answer was before she had spoken, yet let it out as a challenge. Normally, the conversation would have been over, but the amyl had made her lucid and edgy.

'Why not?'

'Because we got something else to do.'

'Who made you boss?'

'I drive.'

'It's Skip's car.'

Skip, quiet now, stayed in the shadows and said nothing.

'Let's go,' Dave said, stepping over Paul and climbing up to the road. Skip followed. Paul stood but did not move up the hill. Rene knew that if she decided not to go, he'd stay with her. And if she went, he'd go. She stood, waiting for Paul to get ahead so that he could help her past the tricky spots.

As it turned out, Dave had nowhere in particular in mind when he'd contradicted Rene. After half an hour of driving up and down the business loop, he swung down a side street into the subdivision. At the first stop sign, he turned off the engine, the radio and lights, and threw a silent fit. He held tightly to the wheel, pulling himself back and forth until the car rocked with him. He then spun quickly in the seat and slapped the side window with an open hand. It made a strangely soft noise that sounded nothing like violence. The others remained quiet, unsurprised and patient.

'Let's go to the Gardens,' Paul said after a while.

Dave said nothing, which meant yes. He started the car and turned right, driving gently. Skip reached over and flicked on the radio. The DJ, an Indian girl named Gazelle, was laughingly reading a newspaper account of a Chinese medical student who was declared a model hero after he drowned in a vat of human excrement while attempting to rescue an elderly peasant.

Anders Gardens were on the estate of the family that had built Research Park around their giant electronics firm. It had once been a sort of rustic paradise, almost European – a forty-two-room mansion situated on hundreds of lush acres, surrounded by marsh and meadow but still close to the city. Scandal and taxes had long since forced the family to sell most of the land to real estate developers, turning the large house and sculpted gardens into incongruous neighbors to splitlevels and public schools. The house itself had become a furniture museum, the various factions of the family moving to penthouses in the city or condos down south. Its only inhabitants now were bored housewives passing an afternoon with out-of-town guests and participants in the inevitable workshops in poetry and silkscreening. The Gardens were maintained by the town as a park.

Dave parked in a side street, unable to get into the chained parking lot of the estates. They had to find their way to the garden's center through a series of unlit hiker's paths, strewn with pine needles and pebbles. The oak and birch trees bordering the paths had been thinned somewhat by the recent cool spell, so they had enough light to find their way. Paul led, Rene next to him, with Dave just behind. Skip brought up the rear. He had become eloquent with a surplus of vodka and drugs, and began to tell the story of the scandal that had split the Anders family and eventually caused them to abandon the estates.

'This was back in the twenties, when the Anders owned everything out here. Well, the heir, P. Piers Anders the Third, was catching a lot of shit on account of his boyfriend, this artist from the city named Lorenz. They lived pretty wild and spent all young Piers' trust fund money on opium and champagne and cruises to Havana. Well, old P. P. number one and Piers junior got wind of it and threatened to cut him off if he didn't dump this Lorenz and settle down with some rich girl they'd picked for him. Well, Piers chose love over gold, but poverty didn't sit too well with them. So one night they swore this pact or whatever and came down here with a brace of antique pistols and a poem about jail by this fag Oliver Wilde and a bottle of *real* Napoleon brandy. Well, Piers did it, right through the heart, but this Lorenz chickened out. Or maybe he never planned to do it. Anyway, the next morning they found the pistols, one fired and one not, the poem and Piers' body with this sarcastic garland of flowers on its chest. The painter and the brandy were gone for good.'

A picture of the scene flashed in Rene's mind. Maybe Piers hadn't died right away, but held on long enough to realize that he had been betrayed. Long enough to see his friend's gesture. In an instant, perhaps, everything that had been precious to him had been made meaningless. His entire life was changed, and changed again. Three lives in the panicked skip of a heart.

The center garden covered nearly an acre, a squat maze of plants only a handful still in bloom in the autumn chill. The complex design of the garden was interrupted periodically by small copses of transplanted lilac and trellised huts covered with wisteria and roses. In the middle of the maze was a large fountain, in whose midst stood a statue of the first Anders, Nordic and resolute under streaks of bird shit. A half-dozen cherubs stood at the fountain's edge, facing inward, benignly gripping their tiny marble penises in a vague salute. Rene figured that the effect was probably different when the water was turned on.

She ducked into one of the covered benches facing the fountain. She had been here dozens of times in the daylight, but never at night. It was good like this, where it had always been unbearable to her before. Now, shadows rubbed out the opulence and made the careful geometry of the maze imprecise, haphazard. She began to laugh.

Skip had perched on the fountain, back to back with a cherub, a few feet above a matted bed of azaleas. Rene could hardly distinguish between them but for the fading arc of urine Skip directed over the foliage. He jumped down when he had finished and began to switch around the small plastic signs that identified each group of flowers. The first he plucked was from a vine near the azaleas he'd just finished watering.

'Rhododendron . . . azalea; now becomes . . . '

Dave stood on the far side of the fountain from Rene, just to the left of the trellised enclosure which balanced hers. He looked comical to her, standing aggressive and confused amid row after row of blossomless flowers.

'*Camassia esculenta* . . . Indian hyacinths,' Skip read, replacing that indicator with the first one.

Dave stared uncertainly at his hands clenched in front of his chest. Then, as if somebody had thrown a switch, he began to thrash around maniacally. He tried to pull down a trellis, but cut his hands on the rose pricks. He pulled at wisteria but it slipped from his grasp like a greased rope.

'*Triteleia uniflora* . . . Starflowers.'

He began to kick violently at the sparse foliage around him, but the kicks were too hard, too poorly aimed to do any damage. He almost slipped down with his final kick, catching himself awkwardly on a small tree.

'*Dicentra luxuriant* . . . Bleeding heart.'

He reached down the trunk and tried to pull up the tree, but the roots would not give. So he began to work it back and forth, still managing only to snap some of the smaller shoots. Rene was laughing loud enough to be heard throughout the garden. Her voice was so bitter, so mocking, that it sounded strange, almost inhuman to her. Dave stopped and stared at her.

'*Erythronium americanum* . . . Dogtooth violet.'

'David. Up here.'

Paul had wandered to the far end of the garden. Rene leaned forward to see. He was gesturing toward the greenhouse, one of the largest in the state, full of rare and exotic flowers. It was bordered by doorless rest rooms and topped by an abandoned aviary. Dave began jogging toward it. Skip remained by the fountain, soundlessly vomiting into a small, chipped urn. Rene stood, but before she started walking noticed a flashlight coming down the path at an angle to intercept Dave. She thought for a moment to call out but didn't, remaining slightly hidden behind the trellis.

The guard was a slight, elderly man, probably a retired policeman from the city. He walked casually to intercept Dave, flashlight bouncing in his hand. Paul had seen him and faded to the edge of the garden. Dave kept moving, jogging with the same intensity with which he drove or thrashed. He didn't really seem to notice the guard until after he had broken his jaw. The old man had begun a bored recital of the garden hours when Dave veered suddenly into his path, pulled a thick stake from the ground and swung it onto the man's face. The stake broke, the top half spinning off into some bushes. The guard seemed to blink for a moment, then fell against a formation of rocks. Dave kicked him in the neck, bouncing his head off the painted stones. The man called out something, then made some low, sucking noises. Dave cocked a leg to kick again, but Paul grabbed him by the shoulders and was leading him from the garden. Rene collected a weak-kneed Skip and followed.

She read signs, counted telephone poles, recalled the lyrics of songs – anything not to think. But the voice had been on too long. Eventually, its intense, hushed monotones penetrated her silence and forced her to listen.

'. . . so again, we only know what we've heard, and that's not much. We've got calls in to the cops and the hospitals and the record company, but again, we've got . . . not gotten ahold of any of them . . . if this is true . . . what it is so far is that somebody called and said they saw him all blue with his tongue hanging out and they put him on an ambulance and took him . . . took Billy Victor . . . to a hospital . . . this was all in front of his East End apartment they said . . . this all just happened . . . we did talk to a nurse at the hospital and she said it looked like drugs and that he was dead but we've heard nothing from the cops or doctors since . . . God, and they just released a new record yesterday . . . '

There was a pause.

'OK, we're going to go to some music now and as soon as we hear anything we'll be sure to pass it along . . . this cut is from the new record, "The Enemy Within".'

Rene listened for death in Billy Victor's voice. It was so fast, so mad – the words seemed to spin away like split atoms, lost as soon as they happened, leaving behind only scars of energy in her mind. Listen, she said to herself. He's dead. Listen.

As they left the Gardens, she had for a moment felt an urge simply to walk the few blocks to her home. But she slid into the car, committed to something she could not understand. Dave, shaking and breathing violently but still

16

driving with care, headed out into the marshlands. He turned off the radio after one song. They sat in their silences.

The marshlands were a barren oval of land south of the city, a horizonless field of low, pale reeds and still pools of purplish water. Covered garbage formed small ridges of hills which broke up the flat monotony of the swamps. Less regularly stood unused electrical substations and powerline trestles, the abandoned brood of a power plant at the marsh's southwest tip, darkened by cost overruns and public protest. The marshlands had formerly been a sanctuary for dozens of species of small animals, but now all that remained were tenacious, ugly birds and a few scavenging mammals. The air was thick with mosquitoes, fireflies and the stink of rotting garbage. The system of shallow, invisible ponds held water too rank and stationary for life.

But it was a good place to drive, possessing a complex and well-paved network of streets awaiting the houses and businesses of the next planned subdivision. Developers, buyers and capital had long since fled south and west, however, leaving a pointless system of sidestreets and cul-de-sacs, a perfect arena for aimlessness.

Rene kept her eyes on Dave. She watched the tense cords of muscle in his neck, his hands clenching and unclenching on the steering wheel, his head nodding obsessively. It occurred to her that she despised him. She wished she could paralyze him, sever his spine and cut off his hands. Hatred welled in her until she was tempted to throw herself against the wheel and turn them into a ditch.

'Let me see your lighter,' she said to Paul. He handed it to her silently, keeping his eyes focused out of the window.

'David,' she said, her voice low and controlled.

He turned around for a moment, then adjusted the angle of the rear-view mirror so that he could watch her. She flipped on the lighter and turned its flame to the highest level. Her head felt lighter than air, buoyed by waves of heat. Now she was there. She dipped the heel of her hand into the flame. Some thin blond hairs turned to hot wire,

17

then disappeared. The flesh began to darken against the flame. Paul was watching her now.

'Stop it,' Dave said, his voice loud.

She continued, her fingers fluttering slightly, her hand remaining steady. The pain felt good. The smell was infinitely sweet.

'I said stop.'

'You can't, David.'

He gunned the engine, accelerating through a hard right onto a side street. The flame bent away from her hand with the car's motion. For an instant, she could see the growing blister, covered with a film of dark blood. The flame straightened back against her hand. Her fingers contracted again with the pain, but she kept her hand steady. Dave was still accelerating. Paul reached over with a rapid and gentle motion, taking the lighter from her. She remained staring at Dave through the mirror, but he had turned his eyes back to the road and was involved with slowing the car.

Skip, weak with nausea and dazzled by the smell, stared at Rene's hand from the front seat. He looked like he wanted to speak, but remained silent for a long time. Rene watched him patiently. For some reason she remembered that his real name was Solomon.

'I've seen her. Gazelle. At the ice-cream shop in the city where all the punks hang out. She's real dark but has light eyes and long fine hair. She was joking with some skins and I could tell by her voice who she was. I asked her to play a song for me that night but Dad was listening to the opera so I don't know if she did. Anyway . . . '

He turned back around and seemed to shrink into the seat. His features slowly hazed over. He closed his eyes against all the spinning, snug in another level.

Rene had sidled over next to Paul and was staring out the window with him, trying not to think about how badly her hand was hurting. She thrust it between her knees, squeezing hard to drive away the pain. Her soul seemed to

18

race off in every direction, leaving her triumphant and strangely content. She watched dying reeds pass and felt like staying where she was forever, clinging tenaciously to night and silence.

But suddenly her tranquility was shattered by a sight that flashed by at the roadside, a vision which lasted for less than an instant yet endured. It burned in her mind, hotter than the flame against her hand – the eyes of some animal lit by the car's headlights, staring right into them: eyes opaque, electric, intent on savagery.

Lighter Than Air

From the back of the line of fidgeting children, James watched his father dispense helium. James sensed how uneasy he felt operating the high-pressure tank, yet also knew that his father, in firmly knotted tie and long sleeves, came across to everyone else as sober and professional as he checked that each balloon received the same amount of gas.

The students lined up in front of James each held a typed postcard explaining that the balloon had been launched from Indian Hills Presbyterian Church as part of a fund-raising campaign and asked whom it may concern to please return the card to the underwritten. One by one, they handed Alan Dole the card and waited somberly as he secured it to the firmly plugged balloon. James was last, so that if the helium should run out he could be among those who would not participate. But there was plenty. He gave his father the card to inspect and then watched as he filled the last balloon. The year before only a few balloons had been returned, so Anders Inc had sent over some small weather balloons for the church to ensure the sort of results they could print in the corporate newsletter. They were as large as beach balls, dark red with clear plastic stoppers.

James and Alan were alone now, the others having run off to the main lawn in anticipation of the launch. Silently, deliberately, Alan filled his son's balloon, the gas hissing between them. They didn't speak, just watched patiently as the balloon expanded to the size of the rest. James stepped up to take it, but his father kept the gas flowing for several seconds, until the balloon's color faded slightly from red to pink. It was almost six inches bigger than the others. Their eyes never met, even as Alan fastened on the postcard and told his son to hurry and catch up with everyone else.

Alan was a deacon in the church, the head of the Sunday schools. He was not a very religious man, but he was a good manager. In the few months following his election, he had employed the most competent members of the congregation as instructors, doubled the funds raised for education and brought in the latest technology to present Bible lessons. Indian Hills Presbyterian was an affluent church, serving primarily as a social and ethical subdivision of Anders Electronics, for which most of the congregation, including Alan, worked. The immense stone sanctuary had been built eighty years earlier with Anders money, its first ministers being superfluous sons of the family. And although both the company's board and the church's ministry were now populated by strangers from prestigious universities, the church continued to serve as a focal point for a series of corporate events.

Like the annual Sunday-school picnic, held at summer's end to mark the students' graduation to the next level. The congregation now gathered on the vast lawns after services, moving through well-orchestrated contests, long tables of home-made food, ceremonies in which everybody seemed to win an award and, finally, through the line to receive their helium balloons. The launch was the climax of the picnic. In the preceding weeks, the students had stalked the subdivision collecting sponsors for their balloons. Each sponsor would pledge a certain amount per mile, usually two or three cents since no balloon had ever gone more than a hundred miles and few were ever recovered. If the card were returned, the balloon's launcher would calculate the distance and collect the amount owed. The money went to overseas missions. Each kid was expected to get about ten sponsors. Intimidated by the prospect of begging pledges, James had gone first to his father, hoping that after that initial pledge he would have the energy to get more. But Alan had said that, being in charge of the launch, he couldn't support his son. It wouldn't be right. After that James had given up. By that Sunday he'd received only one pledge, and that was more or less by accident.

The balloons didn't have strings, so the students gripped them firmly with both hands. James kept his pressed to his stomach, trying to hide its inordinate size. They had grouped in the center of the lawn, their parents forming a vague semicircle downwind. Alan asked if everyone was ready, then began to count down from ten. The students counted along, cried lift off and let the balloons go. They shot up more quickly than anyone had anticipated, rising first as a group, then scattering in the various winds. A few dropped heavily back to earth, skidding across the lawn until they were pinned against the chainlink fence or involved in shrubbery. One bounced into the food tables and burst on a Sterno flame. Most of the balloons, however, ascended rapidly over the trees and houses, picking up speed as they rose into stronger winds.

The children stood still, watching silently, uncertain about what to do with their hands, still raised in release. Some adult began to applaud and everyone readily joined in. James dropped his hands and watched his balloon as it gradually outdistanced the others. He ran to the other side of the church to get a better view. It was soon out of sight. From where he stood, he could see a small group of kids, hiding behind a tool shed, unplug their balloons and inhale the escaping helium. In voices elevated by the gas, they squeaked rapid obscenities and then giggled hysterically.

Someone lit a match and they made a small fire with the address cards.

James' only sponsor was a man named Dan Scales. A week before the launch he had come to dinner at their house, introduced as someone who would be working with Alan in the next few months. His attempts at engaging James in conversation met with no success until, prompted by Alan, he asked about the balloon launch. How many sponsors did James have? None, the boy replied, intent on his plate. Scales asked how much the usual pledge per mile was. Couple cents, James said. Make it a dime, Scales said, smiling broadly at Alan, as if to say that they would soon have more dimes than they would know what to do with. James managed a smile and later wrote Scales in for ten cents.

He was an extremely ugly man, five feet five inches tall, with small thick hands and a bullet head. His stomach burst through his shirt with a hard obesity. His hair was dark and greasy, stretched over a bald spot slightly to left of the top of his head. Dandruff spotted his eyebrows and lashes. His mouth was puffy with large, gapped teeth, some of them capped, one of them dead brown. But he had soft, intelligent eyes that seemed to be capable of great sympathy and a deep voice that immediately took you into its confidence. James' initial feeling of revulsion soon gave way to a strange attraction. It was as if that ugliness disarmed him and caused him to refocus on something more attractive in the man.

He was a consultant who had once worked for Anders but now 'went it alone'. There were many castes within and surrounding Anders Electronics, giving the corporation a structure as densely Byzantine as any medieval city. Of all these castes, the consultants were the most indefinite. They were needed to fill the constantly expanding and contracting form of the corporation, and yet they were free of firm allegiances. James' father, as manager of a research lab, was constantly in contact with these gypsies, working closely with men for several months, then never seeing them again. He had originally expressed contempt for them as parasites but eventually came grudgingly to admit their necessity. He even felt a growing sense of envy for their freedom. Overhearing his meetings with Scales in his study during the days following the balloon launch made James realize just how deep this envy ran, and how thoroughly Scales used it to his advantage.

It was his need for enclosure that put James in a position to overhear his father and Scales. Everything seemed to exhaust him during those days – school, play, eating, the rigors of open space. So he had sought out a series of places where he could rest, closed off and dark places. There was an unfinished sewer in the marshlands, the tool shed behind the church, the cavity under a neighbor's wooden porch. He spent every free moment in these cells. But the late summer heat had killed the air in the hideouts, making them even more exhausting. So he had searched his air-conditioned home and found a small space in his father's study formed by an irregularity in the wall and a row of large bookcases. It was just behind his desk, but James was an expert at silence and was never detected. If he wanted to, he could look through a crack and see his father at work. But most of the time he stayed still and listened to the voices.

Scales often came at night, after dinner. He always told James a joke and sometimes gave him gadgets. James would then slip away to hide himself behind the bookcases as Scales chatted with his mother over the noise of the dishwasher. Scales and Alan would come in and have a drink and joke around for a while, then talk for a long time about the solar collector they were working on. One night, Scales brought it over, a rectangular slab about as big as James, with eight holes on either side. It was made of a hard substance that was as much like glass as it was metal. At first, Alan leaned it against the shelves, covering James' spy hole. The next day James snuck in and moved it slightly.

The men's conversation soon centered on this object, always in language too technical to understand. But later, after they had had a few drinks, Scales invariably tried to convince Alan to leave Anders and work with him. Each night, he put forward the same arguments. Each night, Dole's refusals became less pronounced.

'Listen, Alan, you know I've developed a dozen patents and I don't control a single one of them. Well, this time'll be different. This one I want to keep. Not some dinky two point five commission but one hundred per cent. I mean fifty, with of course fifty going to you. Because I need to make this go, I need your marketing skills.'

James heard his father say that he would be glad to help but couldn't give up his position at Anders.

'Alan, we're talking about the next generation collector here. Look at it. This isn't some modified version that will sell a few thousand units. We're talking about capturing the market here. Not even that, we're talking about creating a market. Ten million gross in the first year with exponential growth after that. All we need is you working with me full time. And that data base from the Anders computer.'

James listened to his father's wavering silence.

'I know Anders, Alan. I used to work there full time, remember? A quarter of the guys there are thinking they can make the Board. And a quarter are maneuvering so that they can leave and get their own things going. And the rest are just treading water. You're clearly among the first group, but tell me, when's the last time somebody from your group even made VP?'

Alan named a name.

'He was promoted at thirty-eight. He was on the fast track, in and out. You've been in research for what, fifteen years?'

Sixteen.

'The way I see it, Anders has found their spot for you. They know good management is hard to find. As far as The Tower is concerned, you are where you belong.'

25

James heard his father admit that he was afraid of as much.

'So let's move. Now. Today. In six months, the technology will have lapped us and one of the big boys will have us. If not Anders then G E or Westinghouse. And we're out in the cold. I'm still a journeyman and you're an aging clerk in the general store.'

After Alan agreed, their conversation became coolly technical. James understood very little beside the changing tone of his father's voice. He was not a man who laughed or shouted – his expressions of emotion were far more subtle. Anger came though in short, rapid phrases and long silences. Satisfaction was expressed by a deliberate, efficient monotone that James heard often during those days. He noticed how his father picked up phrases from Scales and used them confidently, as if he had invented them. Watching him when he was alone, James noticed how he would read and reread the same charts and papers, speaking aloud to himself in an obvious and confidential voice: he noticed his animation when phoning Scales, how he spoke quickly before asking 'How's it going?' And there would be silence as he listened, a silence punctuated only by 'yep' and 'great' and short, fastidious sips from the initialled coffee cup which he more and more frequently filled from the vodka bottle he now kept in his lower right drawer.

On a Friday night three weeks after the launch Scales came by for a quick visit. They decided that it was time to break with Anders. They shook hands, Scales told a joke that Alan almost laughed at. After he left, James watched his father remove a notebook and a bottle from his desk. He read and reread, nodding his head and drinking one stinging sip after another. James sank back into the soft darkness of the enclosure and thought about his balloon. It had been more than a week since the last card had been sent back to its sender. One hundred and eighteen miles. If his card were to be returned, it would have to come from a greater distance. He doubted that it would. The balloon was so fragile, especially with the extra burst of helium his father had pumped in. James imagined the card lying in some field or gutter beside the ripped shell of the balloon, its ink blurred beyond recognition. He tried to stop thinking and get some rest. All he could hear was the periodic click of his father's cup being set down gently on the top of the desk.

The next morning, James' father woke him early and asked him to go to the office with him. It was still dark when they left the house. James had never been out at this hour, never seen the streets of the subdivision so quiet. His father drove very slowly, very carefully, even though they were the only ones on the road. They hit every red light – seven in a row. Each seemed to last an eternity. James thought how easy it would be just to run them. No one would know. But each time they sat and waited for the green as no cars crossed their path, Alan drinking coffee from his initialled mug, James fighting sleep.

It was fully day when they arrived at Anders World Headquarters, a large, windowless building surrounded on three sides by parking lots and fronted by a spacious lawn and reflecting pool. At the back edge of the pool stood a high metal tower with a disk-like top. Alan pointed at it and told him that was where The Board sat. James thought about that for a while but couldn't get his mind around it. They parked in the back lot. The parking lot lights were beginning to click off automatically in the morning sun.

James had never been to his father's office. They entered the building through a dark room full of pipes and dumpsters, then walked down several identical hallways until they arrived at a door with a plaque bearing Alan's name. They entered a small room that contained a couch and an iron desk. James was surprised how cramped and colorless it was. His father explained that this was his secretary's office and he wanted James to sit at the desk and look out for anyone passing in the hall. If he heard footsteps or saw any lights he was to tell him right away. The light was to stay off until he came back. Then he walked into his office. James tried to peer in after him but all he saw was a leather chair and a painting of some clouds.

James slowly swiveled himself in the chair and took inventory of the desk's contents. There was a cup full of pencils and a photo of a man with a moustache. There was a phone with several clear buttons across the bottom, each having a different number printed beneath it, except the last one on the right, which read MODEM. After a few seconds that button's orange light flashed on. James found a small Dictaphone next to the typewriter. There was a flesh-colored wire coming out of it with an earpiece on the end. He fastened it to his ear and switched on the machine. It was his father's voice, droning on about supplies. There were shrill clicks between each sentence. James listened for a while. The room's warm darkness and his father's monotone began to exhaust him. He noticed the space underneath the desk and crawled in.

Perhaps he slept for a few minutes, perhaps an hour. The next thing he remembered was a line of light appearing on the rug, then a man's shoes walking past, into the inner office. His father's recorded voice had finished – all he could hear now was a low electric hum. James pulled the plug from his ear and crawled out of his enclosure. The orange light on the phone flashed out. He walked to the inner door. His father was speaking with an angry, frightened voice that sounded nothing like it had on tape. The other man was even angrier. James didn't know his voice.

He sat back down in the swivel chair, unsure of what to do. After a few minutes the voices stopped and the man emerged from the office. He was tall and wore thick glasses. He walked by quickly, not noticing James. A different button flashed orange on the phone, but went out after ten seconds. James' father appeared.

'I fell asleep,' James said.

Alan just motioned for him to come along. They drove

back the same way they had come, only this time there was daylight and traffic. They didn't speak. Every once in a while Alan would mutter something to himself. As they pulled into their street, he said in a clear voice, to no one in particular:

'Impossible.'

His father shut himself in his study when they got home. James' mother asked him what was wrong and he told her what had happened. She began to look at the closed study door halfway through his story. When he finished he asked her if he'd done something wrong by falling asleep but she simply shook her head.

Alan didn't come out for lunch. James' mother knocked on the door twice but there was no answer, or else there was an answer James couldn't hear. They ate in silence and just as they finished Alan came to the door and asked her to come in. James stayed at the kitchen table, flicking Fritos into his empty soup bowl. He wasn't sure how long it was before his mother came out of the study. She looked at James like she didn't recognize him, then walked to her bedroom and shut the door.

James went out after that, visiting all his usual hiding places. But the thought of his parents holed up in their respective rooms bothered him. It made him feel exposed, like he wasn't alone in his hiding. And that wasn't hiding at all. He went home in the late afternoon and found both doors still closed. He knocked at the bedroom.

'Come in,' his mother said.

He walked in and sat on the edge of the bed. She lay on her back, staring at the ceiling, a gnarled wad of tissue in her hand.

'It occurs to me I haven't done anything for dinner,' she said.

She looked at him.

'Will you do it for me?'

James nodded.

'Your father was fired today, Jamie. Things are going to be a bit different for a while. But don't worry – tonight is the only night you'll have to do dinner.'

James couldn't think of anything to say, so he went into the kitchen. He stared into the refrigerator for a minute but could see nothing he knew how to cook. Then he had an idea. It took him a few minutes of rooting through the drawers until he found the brochure which had been slipped beneath their door a few months earlier. Heavenly Fields Chinese Carry Out. There was a complete menu and a bold-lettered promise of home delivery.

James spent a long time deciding. He was uncertain what the foods were, so he ordered by the sounds of their names, choosing the ones that made him laugh. Maybe that would cheer his parents up. Moo Shoo Pork. Lobster Go Ba. Ling Ding chicken wings. Moo Goo Gai Pan. Lemon Grass. He was surprised when the man he called at Heavenly Fields didn't laugh as he read out the order.

The food arrived a half-hour later. He paid with money he took from his mother's purse, counting it out exactly. The Chinese boy who delivered the food seemed angry when James paid him and it wasn't until his van had squealed away that James remembered he was supposed to tip him. He set the table and put the food in large bowls and went to get his parents. His mother came right away but his father wouldn't respond.

'Let's you and I eat,' his mother said. 'It'll keep.'

Using his funniest voice, James explained to her the names of the food. Once or twice she smiled. They began to eat and Alan came out of the study. He didn't seem to notice the food. He looked as if he'd been sleeping for days – his eyes were heavy, his hair disturbed, his skin pale. James and his mother stopped eating.

'I got through to Jerry Francis. Finally. It all makes sense now. They're hiring Scales as my replacement. That's what this was all about. He wanted his old job back. He was tired and broke and scared of going it alone and so he set me up.'

'But the solar panel,' she said. 'I've seen it.'

'It's useless. I've been looking at it all afternoon. It's a fake. I never thought to check . . . '

There was a long silence.

'What's all this?' Alan asked.

So James went through his litany of funny names, ending with the best – Moo Goo Gai Pan. His father stared at the steam rising from the food. He didn't smile. Maybe I didn't say them right, James thought.

'You'll be hungry again in an hour,' Alan said eventually, scraping back his chair and returning to his study.

During the week that followed, James tried to spend as much time as possible away from home. A weird-looking raccoon chased him from beneath his neighbor's porch and someone locked the tool shed, so he spent all his time in the sewer pipe. It was all right, it had never been used. His parents did not pay him much attention since his father was fired, so he got into the habit of staying there until after dark. That Saturday night a searchlight appeared in the sky. It was the perfect thing to watch as he rested.

His father stayed locked in his study. Occasionally he would go out for a drive and come back with a bottle. He did not bother hiding it from his wife and son. James would run into him in the kitchen or hallway every once in a while. His eyes looked watery and small, as if they had just been scrubbed. But he was still clean-shaven and during the day would wear a tie. He would be cheerful with James but drift off after a couple of words. Once, he patted his son awkwardly on the neck. James' mother told him he was doing phone interviews for a new job. She always seemed to be in the kitchen, drinking coffee, dropping plates.

One night it rained so hard that James had to stay in after dinner. He tried watching TV but all that was on was news. He found his mother playing four-column solitaire in the kitchen and helped her for a few games but they still lost. So he hung around the study's door, waiting for his father.

He came out after a while, walking unsteadily to the bathroom. James snuck in. He was surprised to see the solar panel still there, leaning against the bookcases. He crawled into his place. His father came back and sat at his desk. James noticed that it was completely bare except for a phone and a pad of smudged yellow paper. Alan made a pyramid with his hands in front of his mouth and stared at the pad. After a long silence, he picked up the phone and dialed a number very quickly. He let it ring at least twenty times.

'Son of a bitch!'

James almost called out. He had never heard his father shout before. Alan stood up so fast that he almost fell down. Then he turned around and violently kicked the collector. The shelves rattled around James. His father picked up the instrument and swung it like an axe against the shelves. It began to splinter. The shelves were rattling harder. James felt like running but couldn't move. Finally, his father hit the middle shelf so hard that it fell backwards, landing on the wall and forming a lean-to above him. The other two shelves stood their ground, leaving James plainly visible. His father, breathing heavily, dropped the shattered collector and stared at him.

'I was resting,' James said.

The next day he woke before anybody and quietly left the house. The sewer was ankle deep in rainwater so he decided to wander around the subdivision. He felt strangely energetic. He had not been to school all week and today wasn't going to be any different. He walked to Anders Gardens but they were locked, so he went to the mall and watched the people. They all looked confused. After a while, the smell of hot dogs and roasted nuts made him hungry, so he headed home for lunch. He passed the mailman on their walkway.

'Better pick up your mail, son. It's been sitting there all week.'

His parents had simply forgotten about it. James pulled the letters from the iron box and carried them inside. His mother wasn't in the kitchen, so he tossed them on the table. It was then that he noticed the letter addressed to James Dole, Esq. He never received mail, except on his birthday, much less strange, crinkly envelopes like this. He looked at the stamp for a long time. It said 'Eire'. James' mother walked in and he asked her what 'Eire' meant and she said spell it. So he did and she said she didn't know. He opened it and there was more crinkled paper with handwriting on it, a photo of a place called Galway and his self-addressed card. Only then did it make sense. He went into his father's study. The shelves were upright, the collector gone. Alan did not seem to notice his son. James pulled the atlas from the chipped shelf and laid it on the floor. He looked up 'Eire', learned it meant Ireland and calculated the distance from his house to this Galway place.

'Dad,' he said softly.

'What.' He sounded tired.

'Next time you see Dan Scales, tell him he owes me four hundred and twenty-eight dollars.'

James' father looked at him.

'What?'

James put it all on the empty desk, even the atlas. It took a while for his father to understand, longer than it had taken James. Then he began to laugh. At first, the laughter frightened James. It was so strange, so wild and deep. But it quickly infected him, and he wanted it never to stop. He traced his finger again and again across the blue lines marking the jet stream that had carried his balloon. They were both laughing now, their heads close together, their chests heaving in unison – laughing madly at the impossible.

Alchemy

Oliver Cade pushed his car five miles past the Beltway's limit, then punched on the cruise control. It was going to be an easy trip. The empty predawn roads enabled him to triple his usual speed, giving the commute an exhilarating feel. Dashes of centerline, illumined by the highbeams, raced by his car in fluorescent streaks. He felt his confidence for the eight o'clock news conference rising with the car's momentum. The restless night he had passed fell further and further behind him.

Oliver began to examine himself, anticipating the questions he would be asked, forming the answers he would give. He punctuated his inner dialogue with frugal gestures – a nod, a roll of the hand, a wry smile. The Chairman had told him the day before that a confidential report had been leaked and he should call a press conference for 'damage control'. Oliver knew what that meant. It was the first time since he'd taken the job as company spokesman four months earlier that he'd been called upon to face the press in this way. He'd been handed a copy of the report before leaving the office and, after an initial panic at what it contained, he'd eventually decided that it was deniable. Most of last night had been spent hunched over the legal pad, formulating every question they might ask. Oliver removed his glasses and cleaned them with his handkerchief. No problem, he thought. He could handle this.

Small patches of fog filled depressions in the road, leaving periodic dews on the windshield. Oliver's mind began to wander. The misted glass reminded him of a movie he had seen a long time ago. In the opening sequence, a scientist on a boat passed through a large cloud of fog that caused strange readings on his instruments. Not long after, he began to feel subtle changes in himself, changes that were the beginning of a shrinking process that would end with his becoming so small that he was invisible.

It was just after emerging from one of the small fogs that Oliver saw the spray of sparks on the highway in front of his car, a small flower of flinty blue. As he passed the spot there was a hail of debris against his windscreen – one of the bits of blacktop was large enough to cause a small crack in the glass. Something made Oliver look up at the bridge he was about to pass beneath. A man stood there, outlined by wan, predawn light. Oliver's highbeams caught his eyes, red, like in a cheap photograph. His twisted mouth was surrounded by a strange, stiff-looking beard. The man was in the act of lowering his hands and the last thing Oliver could see before passing beneath the bridge was that he held something straight and dark and dense. He thought for an instant of stopping but told himself not to be foolish. He had work to do.

'Could you repeat that?'

Oliver nodded, trying to see his questioner. His eyes were becoming accustomed to the glare of the TV lights, enabling him to make out some of the reporters. They seemed young, aggressive, hungry for confrontations and rhetoric. Pushing for the one mistake, the one slip that would fill a fifteen-second sound byte.

The Chairman stood hidden in a doorway beyond them.

Oliver did not look directly at him, but could clearly picture the hard, disciplined features of the ex-astronaut: broad chin, slightly outstanding forehead, perfect gray hair. And the eyes, cold and blue like some rare, precious alloy known for its durability and incorruptibility.

'I said, our plan will not cost rate payers a penny,' Oliver said.

It was going well. He'd been at it for ten minutes without being directly challenged. The leaked report had not been mentioned.

'But Mr Cade, if it isn't safe to construct the facility here, how can you in good conscience say it's all right to build it overseas?'

An image of the reactor's design flaws, listed so graphically in the report, flashed through Oliver's mind.

'We don't believe it would be unsafe to construct the plant here, or anywhere else.'

'Then why shut it down? Why sell it?'

'It no longer had the potential for being cost effective in its current, uh, state.'

'A recent UN report describes these sales of nuclear facilities to developing nations as, and I quote, "sowing atomic seeds throughout the globe".'

'Well, that smacks of unwarranted, uh, demagoguery to me.'

Then it came:

'So what about this report we've attained that says the reactor is full of design flaws?'

Oliver paused a moment, making sure his face was utterly relaxed, his lungs full of air.

'There is no such report.'

'Come on, Cade, give us a break.'

Oliver made a short display of keeping his composure.

'I can only tell you the truth – there is no report.'

'So what is this document I've been reading?'

'It's a forgery. Maybe it's a bad joke. There is no report. There is no study. There are no flaws.'

His words seemed to have been said by someone else. He waited for the contemptuous laughter and howls of outrage to begin. Yet there was only the studious scrape of pencils, the whirr of the cameras.

He decided to wrap it up.

'I think you are all overlooking the important role energy plays in the lives of these, uh, people. These countries. As present energy supplies become less and less adequate to growing populations, traditional generating technologies become, uh, obsolete. Nuclear power is essential. We see ourselves as helping these nations develop new, twentieth-century generating cycles.'

'While you reap a huge profit,' came back a voice.

'Anders has nothing against profits. Nor do our stock-holders.'

There was a moment's general laughter. Oliver glanced at the Chairman, who nodded twice, then disappeared. He'd done it.

'Now, if there are no more questions . . .'

A shrill, unfamiliar voice began to speak.

'Isn't it true, Mr Cade, that the Anders logo is associated with pagan rituals, and that it proves your company's use of black magic and other forms of witchcraft to supplement conventional production techniques, and that this proposed sale of the power plant is an attempt to expand your sorcery into the Third World?'

There was a long silence, a few suppressed laughs. Oliver tried to see the questioner's face, but she was hidden in the light. He removed his glasses and polished the lenses. The man's mocking face on the bridge flashed in his mind for an instant.

'Uh, as a matter of fact, we have received a number of calls and letters on this, uh, subject. It appears that some self-styled consumer advocate group has written a ridiculous pamphlet and is distributing it in certain parts of the country. To deny these allegations would be a, uh, cynical farce. Let me just say we trust any rational person can smile at the absurdity of these claims. The use of Mercury's staff as Anders Electronic's logo was intended by our founder to indicate the speed and dexterity with which electricity and its subsidiary technologies permeate and enhance our lives.'

There was brief applause from the reporters, ironic recognition of the skill of Oliver's response. He nodded and collected his papers, signaling an end to the news conference.

He left an hour early that day in order to beat the rush, yet was caught in a long traffic jam on the Beltway's inner loop. Police cars and ambulances occasionally raced by on the soft shoulder, though Oliver could not see the accident. Instead of being angry, he felt magnanimous towards the inconvenience. There seemed to be something deeply graceful about the slow progression of traffic – the way one lane would advance, then another, almost rhythmically. The gracious bows and curtsies with which cars allowed one another to switch lanes. The tempo of turn signals, beating out a measured time. Like a waltz, Oliver thought. The only thing that bothered him was the crack in the window – it had grown a few inches since the morning, as if it were some relentless plant entangling his car. He thought of turning on the radio but decided to slip a cassette of classical music into the player. He turned it up loud, drowning out the sirens that seemed to be sounding on every horizon.

The jam caused him to arrive home a half-hour later than usual. Vince and Dennis came in at the same time, sweaty and elated from the season's first football practice. They had rushed home to see their father on TV. Oliver met them in the garage, thrilling in the admiration they displayed through their jokes and gestures.

Nancy called them for dinner. She said nothing to Oliver when he came in – it was clear she didn't share the boys' enthusiasm about Oliver's new notoriety. He wondered if there would be trouble later. She'd been on him about this job ever since he took it.

They sat around the kitchen table. Oliver said the blessing, then switched on the small black and white. *Happy Days* was just ending.

'So how did it go?' Nancy asked above the music.

'Fine. Just fine.'

She looked across the table at him.

'I watched it on the midday news.'

'Then why did you ask?'

'I just wanted to hear what you thought about it.'

'Nance . . . '

'What, was Dad ugly or something?' Vince asked, food falling from his mouth.

Nancy looked steadily across the table at Oliver. I shouldn't have showed her that report, he thought.

'Speak of El Diablo,' Dennis said, pointing at the TV with his fork.

The local news had come on. Oliver was pictured in a brief clip announcing stories to be featured later in the broadcast. I look good, he thought. Authoritative, credible. But first, the announcer said, they had news of that multiple shooting on the Beltway. Just after dawn there had been reports of sniper fire on the Beltway. Police had launched a big manhunt but had had trouble capturing the elusive gunman, who managed to shoot six people at various locations before being caught in the late afternoon. Traffic was only now coming unstuck. The newscasters were calling him 'The Joker Killer' because he was wearing a cheap costume beard when caught. Oliver stopped chewing. After a few aerial shots of gridlocked traffic they showed a brief photo of the sniper being led to the county courthouse. Oliver recognized the red eyes, the twisted smile, even the plastic beard the policeman held up for the cameras. He thought of the flower of sparks from that morning, of that long, dense thing the man had been lowering as he passed. Oliver put his fork down as he made to tell his family about this remarkable thing, yet when he met his wife's eyes, small and opaque with contempt, he knew that he couldn't say anything she would believe.

Doe

When Frank Tennant saw the taxi turning onto his street, he suspected it had something to do with his son. You almost never saw taxis in the subdivision, certainly not down the cul-de-sac of sprawling ranch homes where Frank lived. It was the sort of street where vehicles only arrived at usual times – after school, rush hours, Sunday mornings. The ice-cream van with its recorded bell, the hissing street sweepers, the Thursday-morning trash collection. Once or twice a limousine to hustle an executive off to the airport. But never taxis.

Yet it wasn't just the cab's novelty which made Frank turn off his weed cutter and wait. There was something else, something that brought his son instantly to mind. For twenty-seven years, everything extraordinary in Frank's life had had something to do with Mark. The mail-order deliveries of seeds or sea horses or teach-yourself-to-draw manuals. The time, when he was fourteen, that Mark had painted a mural on the dining-room wall while they were away on a Caribbean cruise, a tropical scene of waterfalls and giant leaves and brilliant birds that surpassed anything they saw in the islands. They had to hire a man to paint it over. There was the evening two men wearing dirty bandanas walked unannounced into the house at dinnertime and took the television. Mark had kept eating, telling his parents not to disturb the men, that it was all right, it was a debt he had to pay. And, of course, there was the most extraordinary thing of all – Mark's death and cremation in Washington the previous winter.

He had been gone for four years. Their last contact with him had been at his art school graduation, where he and some friends had refused their diplomas and stormed from the ceremony. Frank and Ruth had waited for him in the lobby afterwards, holding rolled programs and the unflashed instamatic, but Mark had never appeared. The next word they had was an anonymous phone call from a vaguely sarcastic voice passing on a rumor that Mark had died in Washington. Frank had traveled there, and, after much waiting in overheated lobbies, had identified Mark from a police photo. He had been found by some railroad tracks six months earlier. Gunshot wound, self-inflicted. No I D. They had run the prints and dental records without any luck. The gun was stolen. They circulated the photo, did a *Crimestoppers*, but no one who knew anything came forward. Frank had asked for the ashes, only to discover that they had been buried in a pauper's graveyard by the Potomac. He went down there and found a poorly fenced tract with weeds as high as wheat. He had stood in the fog for ten minutes, watching birds squabble over a garbage barge which had run aground nearby. He thought he should say a prayer but all he could think of, watching those ugly birds, were Jesus' words about feeding the sparrows.

The taxi stopped in front of his house and a young black woman emerged. She had short hair and full lips, and wore a brightly colored wraparound dress and woven sandals. She walked boldly up the lawn, giving Frank a strong, shy smile. He found himself looking away. She stopped in front of him.

'Man say it's thirty-five dollar,' she said.

'You sure you have the right place?'

The taxi's engine revved.

'Are you Mr Tennant?'

Frank nodded slowly. The driver sounded his horn. Mrs Parker across the street came to her window.

'Does that include tip?' Frank asked as he patted his pockets, even though he knew his cash-stuffed wallet was in his back left.

The woman spread her hands. Frank took the wallet from his pocket and found two twenties. She walked back down the lawn and paid the driver, who helped her take a battered suitcase and a large portfolio case from the trunk. Frank recognized the portfolio as the one he and Ruth had bought Mark for a birthday. It didn't occur to him to help her carry the bags up the lawn. When she reached him she looked at the pile of rootless chopped weeds at Frank's feet.

'This way, you'll have to cut them again,' she said.

'I'll cut them again.'

They waited through a silence. The midsummer dusk was slipping into night.

'Who are you?'

'Ah. O K. I'm your daughter.'

The taxi pulled away. Mrs Parker watched.

'We'd better go in.'

Frank took the bags from her when they reached the kitchen, even though he didn't know what to do with them. He placed them on the tiled floor.

'Do you want some coffee? It's decaffeinated.'

'I have tea.'

'I don't think there is any,' Frank said, making to look in the cabinets he knew were empty of tea.

'It's O K,' she said. She stepped out of her sandals and walked from the room, her now bare feet softly slapping the linoleum. Frank heard the front door open. She returned a minute later with two handfuls of dandelions. She dropped them in a pot she took from the dish rack, then covered them with water and placed the pot on a burner.

'I didn't know Mark was married,' Frank said.

She watched the pot, nodding, saying nothing. There was a long silence.

'Do you know why he didn't tell us that?'

'No.'

'He never spoke about us?'

'Only sometimes. In a way which made me know he didn't want to speak of you.'

'So how did you find me?'

'It was hard.'

'I don't . . . ' Frank said with no intention of finishing the sentence.

The water was boiling now, splattering occasional drops on the high flame. She found two cups without asking, filling them with deft splashes that kept the weed stalks from falling in.

Frank sipped tentatively.

'Too bitter for me,' he said, pushing the cup away.

She was drinking.

'What's your name?' he asked.

'It's hard to say it. Mark just called me Grace.'

'I'm Frank.'

'Frank,' she said, sipping.

'Where are you from, Grace?'

'I'm from him. You know.'

'No. Before that.'

She shrugged and sipped, her eyelids closing. There was a long silence. All the questions he wanted to ask her passed through Frank's mind.

'Are you hungry?' was all he could say.

'The bus stopped on the way.'

'Are you tired? Because you can stay here tonight if you would like to.'

'O yes, I will.'

★

44

He gave her Mark's room to sleep in. It was adjacent to his. Until late at night he could hear the scrape of moving furniture, the rumble of drawers. In the morning, when she was in the bathroom, he put on his robe and went to look. He felt a pulse of anxiety. She had taken down Mark's things – his posters and photos and bulletin board – and stacked them in a corner. The furniture was arranged more efficiently, making the room look bigger. Through the open closet door he could see brightly colored clothes. He wondered where Mark's black ones were.

'Good morning.'

Frank turned. She was wearing a towel fastened beneath her arms. There was a vaccination mark on her shoulder. Frank looked back into the room.

'Making yourself at home, I see,' he said.

'Yes,' she said matter-of-factly. She edged by him, letting the towel fall to her waist. A chevron of scarification covered her lower back, four wedges of black across her brown skin. Drops of water clung to the rough hedges of dead flesh. Some fell as she dried her hair. Frank shut the door and let her dress.

It was the day he made the rounds of his auto parts stores. Though retired, he was still the majority owner. He liked to make his presence felt. He thought about skipping today, but was uneasy about staying in the house with her. Her watchful silence made him self-conscious, a feeling that living alone had nearly purged from him. And he couldn't yet bring himself to ask her about Mark. He wondered if he was afraid of the answers. So he asked her to go with him. She didn't even answer, just got ready. Frank watched patiently as she put some purplish blush along the crests of her cheeks. He didn't know black people used makeup. He'd never thought about it.

They set out at 9.30. He was worried at first about how he would explain her, but decided to make it seem as if her presence were so natural that to wonder about it would be insulting. He headed to the store on the business loop first. It was his newest and largest. The most impressive.

Nate Finlator was up front, showing some new girl how to run the coded cash register.

'It'd be easier if I could just enter the price,' the girl was saying when Frank and Grace approached.

'Morning, Nate,' Frank said in a gently hectoring voice.

'Hello, Mr Tennant,' Finlator said, taking off his glasses and placing them in the leather holder fastened to his left breast pocket. His eyes flickered over Grace.

'So how goes it?' Frank asked. 'I enjoyed your July sheets.'

'July's looking good.'

'July's always good.'

'Summer's always good.'

'Well, August.'

'Yeah,' Finlator said with some bitterness, as if taking it personally. 'August.'

'What is this?' Grace asked. They turned to her. She was holding a brochure advertising prices. In the upper-left corner was a stylized drawing of a coyote wearing coveralls and holding a wrench.

'That's the company motto,' Finlator said.

'Not motto, Nate. Logo.'

'What is the animal?' Grace asked.

'It's a coyote. They're like a cross between a wolf and a dog.'

'A wolf is a dog,' the girl by the register said.

Everyone looked at Grace. She was staring closely at the drawing, tracing its lines with her finger.

'It's him, isn't it?' she said. 'That smile.'

Nate and the checkout girl looked at Frank.

'He drew it,' Frank said softly, taking the paper from her and looking at it as if he'd never seen it before. 'It was the summer before his last year at college and he wouldn't work. Just sitting around his room with those headphones on.

46

Day after day, drawing and drinking quarts of beer. So I came up with the idea that he could draw a logo for the store. This was a time when we were losing a lot of business to Pep Boys so I thought something snappy would, you know. Gave him a hundred dollars for it. And he came up with this and so we went with it and by damn sales edged up.'

'Edged!' Finlator said too loudly.

Frank snapped out of his reverie.

'I told him I'd ask around for more work at the Chamber of Commerce but he wasn't interested, of course,' he said. 'It's a shame because it's so . . . it's not like that other stuff he did. And then he went back to school and, well, here. Take it.'

He handed the paper back to Grace. She placed it on the counter.

They stopped at a supermarket on the way home. Without them discussing it, she did the shopping. She bought things he'd never noticed during his weekly visits – broad leaves of limp kale, shriveled red peppers, palm oil from the gourmet section, a styrofoam bucket of turkey necks she had the butcher fetch from behind the mirrors. He'd never spent so little for so much.

'Do you cook?' she asked when they were in the car.

'Not much. Fish fingers. Stuff like that. Birdseye. Ruth did the cooking.'

'And where is Ruth?'

'She left. Couple months ago.'

'Left?'

'Right.'

Frank smiled at the unintentional pun. He looked at Grace. She hadn't caught it. They drove for a while, following a TransAm whose license plate read *Big Mony*. Grace pointed at it.

'Everything here is signs. You know. T-shirts. Billboards. Buttons with the smiling faces. People talk through signs.

Everyone you meet has a sign which you must read. Have you noticed this?'

'Not till now.'

He looked at her, thinking for a moment of the scars on her back. He wanted to ask her about them.

'I'd never seen him in that drawing before,' he said instead.

'O he's there.'

'Can I ask you something?' Frank asked as he slowed for a yellow light. 'Why weren't you there? I mean, why didn't you identify the body? They said they held it for ninety days.'

She rubbed the dashboard's worn vinyl.

'I went there. They showed me him and his gray face with the sewed-up hole above the ear. They wanted to know who it is and I tell them I don't know.'

She cooked all afternoon, seeming to know where everything she needed was. He cleared the Japanese beetle traps in the cherry and crab apple trees in the back yard, emptying the dead insects into a clear plastic bread bag. Some were still alive and he killed them by flicking off their heads with his forefinger. As he worked, he wondered what he was going to do with her. She couldn't stay, that was for sure. It wasn't just the impracticality of it, the oddness of it. There was something else. Those scars.

She was standing on the porch, staring at him. He replaced the last trap on a branch and walked slowly back to the house, dropping the bag on a deck chair.

Whatever was cooking was cooking hard. She was using a pot he'd forgotten they had, a large steel tureen Ruth had used to boil down fruit for preserves. Steam clouded the windows and moistened the wall above the stove. There was a strong vinegary odor. He sat at the table, which had been set with paper towels and large serving spoons. She loaded two plates with mounds of starched rice, then covered them with stew from the steel pot. The kale was in a bowl.

'Good,' Frank said, wincing at the food's spicy heat. Fat-shrouded turkey spines, smoking peppers, clots of rice. The kale so sour he had trouble swallowing. He poured himself another glass of ice water.

'This was Mark's favorite meal,' she said.

'I thought it was mushroom chicken.'

'What's that?'

'Something Ruth made. I don't know. You roll up a chicken breast and then pour mushroom soup over it.'

Grace dismissed this with a gentle nod.

'Why did Ruth leave you? It seems everyone leaves here.'

Frank pulled a spine from his mouth.

'She went to live with my brother Val,' he said, scrutinizing the meatless bone.

She looked at him.

'Your brother.'

'Yes. She had gone with him before we were married but then Val got married to a girl from New York. Dumped Ruth just like that.' He snapped the bone. 'So she married me. Linda – Val's wife – died of septicaemia two years ago and after we heard that Mark was gone Ruth just sort of went back with Val. She went to keep him company and stayed on, this is what I tell people. There wasn't any big deal about it. It felt very prearranged, although of course nobody knew that it was. Do you know what I mean?'

'Yes.'

'So how did you and Mark meet?' he asked after a while.

'At the restaurant. He was a waiter. I bussed.'

Frank waited.

'He used to make fun of me. The way I talk. But he would help me clear when he wasn't busy. That was kind. Then he took me to a Japanese restaurant. You take your shoes off. We fed each other. You know. I stayed with him and when my visa ran out he married me.'

Frank poured two more glasses of water.

'He stopped at the restaurant and I got a job at a nursing

home. Private care. Changing old people's diapers. A hundred dollars a day.'

Frank raised his eyebrows.

'His work went bad. Nobody bought it. He tried painting on different things. He began to work with tools. I didn't understand. His paintings became ugly.'

'I thought so too, some of them.'

Frank wanted to ask her about the days leading to Mark's death but instead asked her where she was from.

'Liberia.'

'I don't know much about that.'

'It's in the west of Africa. Many of the people there are descended from slaves from America who went back. Not my people, though. They were never slaves. They were always there. And when the slaves came back they took us over. You know?'

'Happens.'

'Maybe you remember the men on the beach. They tied them to stakes and put hoods over the head and shot them. There were pictures in the world press.'

'O yeah. I remember that. Few years ago, right?'

'A man named Samuel K. Doe became president. So I left. You know.'

'Doe. That's what they called Mark after he died. John Doe.'

She nodded, as if this made perfect sense. Frank stopped eating.

'So what are your plans, Grace?'

She shrugged.

'What I'm trying to say is that I don't think you can stay here.'

Grace stared into her plate.

'I mean, you can stay for a while and then you can visit but I don't think you can live here.'

She said nothing.

'What about your people? Can't you go to them?'

'People?'

'Family. You know.'

She looked confused.

'But I'm your daughter.'

'I'm afraid I don't see it that way, Grace.'

'What do you mean, see it?'

'What I mean,' Frank said, 'is that I don't know about you. I don't know about this situation. You show up here and you say you're his wife and, well, there are questions, that's what I'm saying. Why did Mark kill himself? Where were you when it happened? Why didn't you do something about the body? At least give him a name so they could have called me. But instead I have to hear he has no relatives, he was alone. So they bury him a pauper. John Doe. And now I find out there's a wife? Excuse me?'

'I said I was with a friend.'

'What does that mean?'

'I had gone to live on the couch of my friend.'

Frank thought about this for a minute.

'So you'd split up. Fine. So you were through with Mark and when he died you couldn't bring yourself to do the decent thing. Fine. That happens. So what makes you think you are my daughter?'

She looked him in the eye.

'We hadn't split apart. I was hiding from him. By the time I was brave enough to go back he was dead. I didn't tell anyone because I was ashamed.'

There was a long silence.

'You were hiding from him?' he asked softly. 'Why?'

'Because he hurt me.'

'How?' he asked, the word strangled by his reluctance to know. She just stared at her hands, as if he hadn't asked at all.

Frank looked at the yard. The gusting wind had knocked some of his traps from the trees. He wondered where bugs went in weather like this.

'OK,' he said. 'All right. You can stay some more.'

★

That night he awoke to flames reflected on his wall. He walked to the window overlooking the back yard. A fire burned in the barbecue grill at the end of the porch. Its heat moved the leaves of a nearby tree. Grace was there, placing a large sheet of paper on the fire. Frank checked the clock. Almost 4 am. He put on his robe and went out to her.

Mark's leather portfolio case was open on the lawn. She fed in the canvasses slowly, waiting until one burned before introducing the next. The oils flared hot and blue.

'Destroying the evidence?' he asked, immediately wishing he hadn't. She didn't understand his humor.

'They burned him so I thought I would burn these. You know.'

Frank walked onto the porch, fetching the plastic bag from the deck chair. He poured some of the dead beetles into the grill. In the fire their movement mimicked flight.

'There'll only be more,' she said.

'I know.' He pointed at the portfolio. 'Are you going to burn them all?'

She nodded a little.

'Can I see them first?'

She didn't move.

'When we first met he would sketch me. At the restaurant, at home. In the morning. As I cooked. Always. Just simple drawings, one line, pencil never leaving the paper. You know. He did one on a napkin, one on the donut bag. I said why are you drawing me? And he would say because you are a beauty. Man, no one has told me that, ever. I know he believed it because he put it down on paper. A whole book of paper.'

'Are these them?'

'No. He destroyed all those last summer. These are the later ones.'

'Can I . . . '

'Yes, yes, all right. You can see them.'

He picked the portfolio from the nightwet grass. He had to turn his back to Grace and the fire to see the work.

The first canvas was a pencil drawing of a naked woman, spread-legged on a disturbed bed. Her crotch was drawn in a heavier lead than the rest of her body, the vagina a deep black gash. Her head was propped awkwardly on a ripped pillow. It had no face.

The next piece was smaller, its edges torn. The paper was streaked with vivid colors, like a child's fingerpainting. In the middle was an 8 × 10 photo of Grace, seated naked in a chair. Her firm breasts were sketched over in red tempera to make them look like a hag's hanging dugs. Yellow, worm-shaped strands obscured her crotch. Her lips had been smeared by real lipstick.

The next work was another photo, this one a close-up of Grace asleep. A section of the photo's surface, over her chin and lips, was coated with a glistening, glue-white crust. A ballpoint doodle marred the upper-right corner: 'Fuck pig.'

Frank flipped through several more photos and canvasses, stopping at a large watercolor portrait of the two of them. She was dressed in an ornate West African costume and seated on some sort of wicker throne. She looked regal, powerful, just as she had when Frank first saw her striding up the lawn from the taxi. Mark stood next to her, his naked body sallow and disproportionately small. He had a hunched back and a penis like a tiny rotting bud. His eyes stared out of the painting with a glazed, dead look. His mouth had a twisted smile like the coyote in the ad.

Frank turned around. Grace had gone indoors. A searchlight beat through the sky beyond the house, a sight that made Frank suddenly feel very small and very alone. He began to put the rest of the paintings into the fire, one at a time. Charred beetle corpses tumbled into the glossy cauldrons of the melting photos.

She slept late. It was a funny day – bursts of rain, followed by intervals of brilliant sun. When he went for the mail

Frank could feel cold and warm currents intermingling in the gusts. The radio mentioned a tornado watch a few counties away. Grace was at the kitchen table when he returned.

'Do you want some breakfast?'

She said nothing. Her eyes were puffy. He sat opposite her, fanning out the mail like a card dealer.

'The funny thing about Mark's craziness was how it came to be the only real bond between me and Ruth,' Frank said after a while. 'You'd think it would be the sort of thing that would drive a couple apart, but on the contrary. We used to huddle together beneath his attacks, so to speak. I'm sure that's why she's with Val now that he's dead.'

He shuffled through the mail.

'One night, Ruth and I were making love, and just as I finished I was aware of his presence. He was standing in the darkest corner of the room. Don't ask how long he'd been there. He wasn't so young at this time. Fifteen. Then Ruth noticed him. We all looked at each other and then he just sort of snorted and walked from the room. We both felt very ashamed but the funny thing is we made love again just a few minutes later, which is something we never did. Never. And it was so, I don't know, close.'

He looked across the table. She was crying silently.

'How can somebody hate themself, Grace? Can you tell me? I could never get my mind around that. Hating us, me and Ruth I mean, I could have accepted that in the end, even though it hurt. But having him hate himself and now him dead . . . '

Something was tapping at the window. Small, fine balls of ice. She looked up.

'What is that?'

'Hail.'

'I don't know about that,' she said.

'It's ice.'

'Ice? No. It's summer.'

'This happens.'

'I have to see.'

She stood, slipping from her sandals, her feet gently slapping the floor as she walked to the back door. Frank watched through the window as she ran into the yard, holding up her palms and squinting into the sky. She stuck her tongue out, then looked at him, smiling. He nodded. She began to turn slowly, her eyes closed.

There was a violent pulse of wind through the trees. The hail came harder, bigger. Some of the marble-sized stones shattered upon hitting the concrete porch. They created small colored prisms as they melted, reminding Frank of the designs Mark used to make with the Spirograph they bought him for his sixth birthday. He would give them to Frank as presents, but not before insisting that the previous drawing was torn into small pieces. Frank hated to do that because they were so beautiful.

The hail fell even harder. He remembered Grace. She was no longer spinning, but had hunched over, recoiling as large stones struck her. Her splayed fingers wriggled frantically over her temples and ears. She looked around to run but had lost her bearings. All she could do was remove her blouse and shield her head with it. Frank saw the neatly formed scars on her back.

She was on her knees by the time he reached her. He lifted her by the shoulders and led her to Mark's bedroom, where he wrapped her in a blanket. He sat with an arm around her shoulders for a minute until she stopped shivering. Then he slowly pulled the blanket from her and looked at the scars. They shimmered each time she sobbed. He traced them with his fingertips. They felt like flawed rubber.

'Did he . . . '

'Did he what?'

'He did this to you, didn't he?' Frank asked.

She stopped crying and looked at him. She pulled the blanket over her shoulders.

'No. They were done when I was a girl. So I could become a woman. They are for my beauty.'

Frank leaned forward.

'I thought he . . . ' he whispered.

'No, no.'

'Because they are so beautiful.'

Half-Life

The evening shoppers reminded Laura of animals foraging on a desolate plain. They scurried among the stores in tight, rapacious groups, sniffing at Italian shoes or fireplace supplies, scattering if approached by salespeople. The occasional loner darted by at a halting, reptilian pace – clutching a purchase, checking the time, glancing into the stores without stopping. Few spoke, yet the mall was filled with a collective, almost inhuman din.

None of these creatures were stopping at Laura's stand, a small oasis of handmade jewelry situated in the concourse between the long rows of shops. She watched them pass with a solicitous, clinical contempt, waiting only for closing time. Most of her sales came in the late afternoons to schoolgirls or housewives killing time before having to be home for dinner. The evening shoppers would simply pass her stand with blank, purposeful glares.

It did not matter to Laura that she wasn't selling. She paid only a nominal rent, and all of her stock was taken on consignment. The aging hippies who supplied her with the clay earrings and teakwood necklaces would drive in from farms up north every other Friday in their vans and station wagons, smelling of woodsmoke and pot. They were not demanding. Laura envied their freedom and indifference, sometimes thinking how easily she could join them, with her long straight hair, natural clothes and face free of cosmetics. Just take off with them. Maybe with that brooding carpenter, Colin, or the two lesbians who always finished each other's sentences. But no one asked. They would wordlessly collect their fees and leave quickly, as if the atmosphere in the mall were poisonous to them. They seemed to care as little about the money as Laura. Breaking even was enough.

At eight o'clock, an hour before she closed, Laura turned on the small television her husband had bought her when she'd complained of tedium. It was permanently tuned to PBS. This was her favorite hour of broadcasting, when shows dealing with science and nature were aired. Tonight was the last episode of a documentary about the recently discovered tomb of Ch'in Shi-huang Ti, Builder of the Great Wall, Burner of Books, and the First Emperor of China. Laura slumped in her folding chair, hoping no one would stop at her stand.

As a young prince, the show explained, the future Emperor had turned the small, fertile state of Ch'in into a lean, disciplined war machine that easily defeated its softer neighbors. Before he was forty, Ch'in Shi-huang Ti had unified a disparate, feudal association of states into what is now modern China. The next nine years were spent imposing a brutal code of law upon his people. Power soon produced megalomania and paranoia in the Emperor. A supposed threat from northern nomads was met by the construction of a wall 1,864 miles long. A rumor of dissension among Confucian scholars led to 460 of them being buried alive. Laura was enthralled – she loved facts like this. The most minor transgressions among the populace were punished by dismemberment and death.

Having conquered earth, Ch'in Shi-huang Ti set out to master heaven. He contested his mortality by erasing all recorded history predating his birth. Books containing evidence of this time were burned, old men who dared recall it had their tongues cut out – and Ch'in's mother, ultimate evidence of his mortality, was banished, some say even killed.

As he grew old, alchemists, sorcerers and mystics were brought to court to help prepare the Emperor for immortality. Emissaries were dispatched to heaven to ready its citizens for subjugation. And a tomb was designed to ensure Ch'in's triumphant entry into the other world. Laura watched in awe as the camera panned over the recently excavated army of seven thousand life-sized terracotta statues in attack position that surrounded the Emperor's corpse. Archers, cavalry, charioteers – all poised, as if waiting for their leader's command to storm the heavens.

'How much is this?'

'Four dollars,' Laura said, not wanting to take her eyes from the television.

'Is that all?'

She missed the last minutes of the show making a sale. By the time she could return her attention to the television, credits were showing over close-ups of the terracotta soldiers. Each had an individual face, their expressions ranging from savagery to bemused resignation. She turned off the set as glass doors and metal cages echoed shut around her. The mall's loudspeakers were clicked off in mid-swell of Muzak. She quickly locked her cases, put the strong box in her bag, and headed home.

The next day she and Wade went for their tests. Their appointment was first thing in the morning. Wade took the rest of the day off to get some things done around the house, stopping at hardware and rental stores on the way home from the clinic. Laura decided to bake some bread, sometimes catching sight of her husband through the steamy kitchen window as he removed the cracked and aged paint from the garage. He was using a rented machine that issued a narrow,

59

intense wave of heat, causing the paint to bubble and peel off the old wood. Long strips would drop like multicolored serpents into the weeds at his feet.

Laura smiled wistfully at the fastidious care Wade brought to the job. He used to be so gracefully sloppy, so rumpled and effortless. But now, with his feet spread a bit too wide, his back held perfectly straight and his head cocked so tensely – he looked like one of the more unlikely of the terracotta swordsmen from the documentary the night before. An apprentice, unsure of his weapon. And his spotless workclothes, purplish goggles and white mesh mask further added to his inhuman quality.

His outfit made her suddenly think back ten years, to when they had just graduated from college. They had been hired by a wealthy woman to drive her Cadillac to the West Coast. She gave them a gas credit card, some cash and thirty days. They had zigzagged their way through the country, staying with friends, seeing the sights. In New Mexico, they had met up with Wade's cousin, an occasional student at a state college. He had introduced them to his friends, who were older and used rare drugs. The night after their arrival, the group asked Laura and Wade if they wanted to take part in a protest in the desert. They readily agreed.

After taking a circuitous, backtracking route that struck Laura as ludicrous, they reached the spot, designated by nothing more than a rusty fence bearing a sign that read WARNING: RESTRICTED: US GOVERNMENT PROPERTY. They cut through and, in receding daylight, wandered the mesa, finally establishing camp beneath an abutment to a large formation of reddish rock. Someone built a fire, a bong was passed around while somebody else arranged a neat grid of microdots on a flat rock. A tape player was produced and traditional Hopi music alternated with Jefferson Airplane for the rest of the night.

While the others dozed or tripped, Laura and Wade took their sleeping bag atop the abutment and made love. She remembered his pressure, light and insistent; the coolness of the rock and the way the stars streaked before her fluttering eyes. She remembered a curious lizard watching them and the sound of dry wood cracking as it burned below.

The next morning they woke to the sound of an approaching vehicle. Squinting in the harsh morning light, they saw a van racing toward them, whipping an angry tail of dust behind it. The people below began to stir as Laura and Wade scurried down the abutment. The van skidded to a stop a few hundred yards away.

'It's cool, man,' the group's leader said. 'They know we're here.'

'Obviously,' Wade said.

'No, I mean, we told them. We left a message.'

Two men climbed from the van. They wore oversized white protective suits with glassy face masks that reflected the early morning sun. They stared at the group, passing a pair of binoculars between them.

'It's Buzz and Neil,' Wade's cousin said, causing only nervous laughter.

One of the men began to wave his arms above his head, then pushed his hands toward them, beckoning them to retreat. The other read some sort of portable meter. The two men stopped and stared for another minute, then drove off.

'They were just trying to scare us,' the leader said.

'It worked,' Laura said shakily.

'Maybe we'd better go,' Wade said.

'All right. Don't worry. They knew we were here. We left a message.'

Laura cleared the condensation from the window, and it was as if she'd wiped the memory away as well. Wade had moved around to the far side of the garage. The clean wood steamed from the machine's heat.

The next evening, Laura didn't bother going to the mall. While waiting for Wade to return from the doctor, she searched the attic for their camping equipment. She found a tent, a hurricane lamp and one sleeping bag. She wiped as much dust and mildew as she could from the cloth and lugged it all into the back yard. She pitched the tent near the hedge at the back.

Dr Williams had called Wade at work, asking him to come to the clinic. Laura was scared. They had both undergone the fertility tests, so why had Williams asked only Wade? It could be that it was him and the doctor wanted to break it to him alone. Or that it was her, and Williams wanted to let Wade break the news. It could be both of them. Or neither. It could be anything.

It was dark by the time she'd set it all up. Fireflies began to float up from the long grass and settle in the tent's soft canvas. She sat crosslegged on the mouth of the tent and watched a spotlight that was cutting across the sky. For some reason it made her think of that lonely Emperor believing he could storm the heavens.

She thought back to when they had first moved to the subdivision, a time dominated by a half-bemused, half-ashamed irony that allowed them to treat leaving the city as some sort of joke they were playing on themselves. It was as if everything they did – hanging wallpaper, planning how to beat the Beltway rush hour, joining Neighborhood Watch – was done in brackets, in quotation marks. As if the subdivision were some necessary exile, to be endured with the stoic good humor of gentlemen officers in a POW camp. One day, Wade had returned from Anders in a bad mood and asked her why the chicken crossed the Beltway. Laura couldn't answer, she couldn't laugh.

They stopped the joking and were possessed by a nervous, guilty energy, as if they felt the need to solve a problem or remedy a mistake. Wade put in long hours at his job, roaming the house like a caged animal when he was off. Laura, who was not working, signed up with a local committee to block completion of the nuclear power plant at the far edge of the marshlands.

Most of the people were her age, although there were some students and elderly lawyers from the city. Her first job had been to look after the nursery the committee provided for its members during the meetings. She was then given a canvassing job, ringing doorbells around the subdivision, distributing literature, asking the more sympathetic people for contributions. Most were polite, many even signed the petition.

After a few months, she was promoted to canvass director. She worked out of the house. Wade was still gone all the time, so she was able to convert the kitchen and the den into a command center. Other women began to spend time there, even some students. They all felt energized by the difficult work.

For Laura, these sessions somehow redeemed her spacious house, an aluminium-coated ranch that was younger than her or Wade. There was a standing invitation to everyone on the committee to come by any time between breakfast and dinner. Many took her up on it. The kids got high, there were arguments, drunken confessions, even a brief affair in the guest room between a part-time canvasser and a graduate student from the city. As Laura daily cleaned up the cigarette butts and coffee-crusted cups, she began at last to feel at home with the smell and textures of the house.

It ended suddenly, without warning and seemingly without reason. The phone rang one morning and the committee's senior counsel, a lawyer with long, gray hair and a classical actor's voice, said that the utility had suspended work on the nuke. He told Laura that she and the others should be proud, that they had played an instrumental role in defeating the plant.

Shortly after, Wade had staked her his first bonus to start up the jewelry stand. At first she had actively pursued customers, but soon was just smiling politely at anyone who lingered in front of the cases. She began to take long lunches, sell items at cost. Some days she didn't go in.

And then, as if the last step in some path she'd been

following since that night on the mesa, she told Wade they should have a child. He'd agreed, of course. That was more than a year ago.

Her reverie was interrupted by the sound of a ringing phone. She balanced on her toes, trying to determine if it was theirs. It was. She sprinted up the lawn and into the house, but heard the dial tone when she picked it up. The ringing seemed to echo in the kitchen.

As soon as she returned to her campsite she sensed that something was wrong. She stood still for a moment, staring into the dark tent. The fireflies had flown off the canvas and were again hovering above the grass. There was a soft scratching noise inside, an occasional wheeze. Laura squatted and, her eyes now accustomed to the darkness, made out the silhouette of the animal.

Thinking it was a cat, she rustled the tent flap and said 'Shoo, beat it.' The animal recoiled, putting its chin close to the ground, its rump high in the air. It made a low, menacing sound. Laura took a few steps back. It began careering slowly toward her. It was a raccoon. White froth covered its face, caked blood its paws. Laura stamped her foot but it continued to advance. So she scooped up the hurricane lamp and threw it at the animal. It skipped off the ground and caught it on its flank. The raccoon rolled over once, then fled into the hedge.

Laura watched the rustling bushes, her heart racing. She wanted to run back to the house, but was afraid to turn her back on the animal. Something touched her shoulder.

'Goddamnit!'

She turned so quickly that she almost fell. It was Wade. She saw the shadow of the stiff smile that had just fled his face.

'You scared me, Wade.'

'What's the matter?'

'I was just attacked by a crazed animal, that's what's the matter. Why the hell did you sneak up on me?'

'Where did it go?'

She pointed to the hedge. He looked. She saw he was holding a six-pack, smelled Scotch and mint on his breath. Her anger subsided but her heart continued to pound.

'I'm sorry,' he said, still looking toward the hedge.

'It's all right,' she said softly.

He continued to look toward where the raccoon had fled. She took a beer from the ring and popped the top. The sound brought him back.

'It's me,' he said, exhaling the words, as if just surfacing after too long underwater. 'Or maybe I should say it isn't me.'

Laura felt a pulse of heat race from some core within her to the extremities of her nerves and flesh. Suddenly, she could not look at Wade, though she tried. She couldn't think about it. Strange images entered her mind instead: the serpents of paint from the garage, customers' hands reaching for jewelry, the faces of the Emperor's soldiers. These interloping thoughts soon gave way to a lucid realization of a split in herself, as if one piece of time had just ended, giving way to another. Something in her life had at last become final, and vestiges of her past life had been irrevocably sealed away.

'So what's all this?' Wade asked, gesturing at the camping equipment.

Laura looked at the tent, covered again by fireflies. Then she looked at Wade and wished somehow she could make his beaten expression vanish. But she feared that his face had become a mask, a mold of confusion and defeat that could not be changed, only broken. She spun around and, with a single stroke, knocked the brilliant insects back toward earth.

'A bad idea I had. Come on. It's dangerous out here.'

She took Wade's hand and led him back to their house.

Death of the Libertine

Jack Allen stopped at a red light and brooded over his son's graduation. After having flunked out of two private universities, William had recently coerced a diploma from a third – a sprawling, indefinite urban college attended mainly by adult part-timers and foreigners on student visas. He had gone nights, working in a record store by day. Because he had finished his requirements during the summer session, there had been no graduation ceremony, just coded grades posted on a bulletin board and a voucher which could be redeemed for a diploma sent in the mail.

Jack turned off the radio, where an announcer had interrupted a symphony between movements to ask for donations to a fundraising drive. He shook his head and gave a small, disgusted whistle through clenched teeth. No graduation ceremony signifying a job well done. No gown, no procession, no photographs. Just a computer print-out and a voucher. Important things could not just end that way, without being celebrated and finalized. It gave the event a feeling of cheapness . . .

His thoughts were interrupted by a violent tremor through the front of the car. He immediately thought engine trouble, then realized the disturbance was coming from the road. The car vibrated more violently as a spray of water washed his right side window. Chunks of concrete popped up just before him, giving the road the look of a disintegrating glacier. A van in the lane to his right pitched forward slightly, its front wheels sinking into a depression. Horns began sounding around him, but were quickly drowned out by a menacing hiss. Jack put his car in park and reached for the door.

A water main had broken beneath the intersection. Its contour was described by a shifting mound that ran diagonally through the blacktop. Liberated water bubbled through the broken concrete, shooting up in several small geysers. After a short while, the road stopped trembling, the main's pressure having found sufficient outlet. As water began to flood the road, Jack inched his car through the intersection.

After telling his wife and daughter about his adventure, he retreated to his study and began to make some calls. Within half an hour, he had organized a dinner to celebrate his son's graduation. He told his wife to plan a menu and inform William. Everything was set.

Except for one thing. The gift. He wanted to give his son a gift that carried a message expressing Jack's mixed feelings about the course his life was taking. William's tastes were a mystery to him, so a material present was out of the question. It would have to be cash. But how much? Necessity placed practically no limits on Jack – seven of the nine nursing homes were turning substantial profits, while the others' losses were negligible. And yet too large a gift would send too positive a signal. He had to be sure to temper his pride in his son's accomplishment with an implicit admonition to continue moving forward.

One thousand dollars was the sum he settled upon. It was enough to have a palpable effect on William's life style without enabling any laziness. It would provide an impetus for his son to take hold of his life's reins, to move out of his dingy apartment and find a job with a future. It would be the best possible gift – a catalyst.

The Saturday of the dinner got off to a bad start. Jack's lawyer called before breakfast and said that they were in trouble with a wrongful death lawsuit. The decision would surely go against them. The lawyer wanted to settle out of court. Jack said that was out of the question and hung up. He then received a call from his brother, a dissolute inventor of electronic devices, who said that he and the family would be unable to attend the dinner. He gave good reasons. Jack's wife returned from golf at midmorning and said she'd spoken with William's godparents on the back nine. They, too, gave good reasons.

Jack felt a violent rush of anger. He quarrelled with his wife. He kicked objects. He refused lunch and struck the dogs. When his temper began to abate, he retreated to his study. Amid the unread reports and photographs, he regained his composure. He poured himself a bourbon and called his lawyer.

'David, are we definitely going to lose?'

The lawyer said there was no question.

'What are they asking to settle?'

The lawyer named a sum.

'And what are we offering?'

The lawyer named the same sum. Jack took a sip and then nodded. There was a pause, followed by the lawyer asking if Jack were nodding. Jack said yes and hung up the phone. He continued to nod, watching the men plant shrubs in the yard. Something occurred to him. He straightened up in his chair and opened the top drawer of the desk. He found his checkbook and made out a check for his son. Without thinking, he wrote in two thousand dollars.

After making a few more calls, Jack went out to the yard to check up on the gardeners. They were a team of Vietnamese refugees, a father and three sons whose stylized work had

68

become fashionable in the subdivision. Jack had hired them to build a wall of shrubbery to enclose the backyard. He found the father working alone, patting soil around the bush.

'Where are the boys?' Jack asked genially.

Without turning around, the old man made a jabbing gesture with his left hand, as if describing the ascent of some bird. Jack did not understand what it meant. He stood motionless for a while, watching the old man work. Something didn't seem right about the hedge.

'Are you sure this is right?'

The man stopped working and patiently looked over the row. Then he looked somberly at Jack.

'This good.'

'Not too deep?'

'This good.'

'The roots won't get sogged?'

'This good.'

'Are you sure?'

The old man answered with silence. Jack felt a rush of anger. He strode to the other end of the row, squatted before a bush and began to wrench it from the ground. It was so firmly embedded that it took a tremendous effort to expose the roots. He felt the Viet's presence behind him.

'This good,' the old man said, making a jabbing gesture with his left hand. He then walked slowly to his truck and drove away.

Sweating copiously, Jack stared down into the hole he had created. Amid the dark soil and severed roots was a colony of strangely luscent insects, like so many pieces of tangled thread. They had gray, viscid cores surrounded by a reticular white film. A dozen or so frantically wriggling legs issued from the bodies. The early afternoon light seemed to be causing them immense pain – perhaps killing them. Jack was fascinated by these creatures he had never before seen. He continued to watch as, one by one, they stopped moving. When the last fell still, he gently covered them with a layer of peat, set the shrub back in its hole and returned to the house.

He poured himself some bourbon and turned on the television. It was on the rock video channel. Jack pointed the remote control at the set and pressed the 'mute' button. The screen showed a band playing in a small, dingy club that was packed with savagely dancing kids. The band's singer lunged periodically toward them but was restrained by a chain attached to a dog collar around his neck and bolted to the floor. Streaks of spit and half-empty plastic cups rained continuously upon him. Jack clicked off the television, sprawled on the couch and fell asleep.

He was jolted awake an hour later by the vague feeling that he had a tremendous task to undertake and only a short period of time in which to complete it. He stood in the empty room, sweating heavily, his heart racing. It occurred to him that it was only the dinner.

He found his daughter seated at his desk in the study, speaking on the phone. She had twisted the cord into a half-dozen loops around her hand and was rhythmically stretching the coils.

'Yes, I think once we can bring the message to them, they will no longer feel the need to smoke drugs or drink beer, which is what leads to it, don't you think? It's just a question of . . . '

'You'll ruin the cord,' Jack snapped.

She looked at her father.

'Alice, I'll have to go now. I'll see you tonight, all right? God bless.'

She hung up the phone.

'Dad, I can't make William's dinner. They've called a special Young Life meeting for this evening. About teen pregnancies. The state supervisor's coming and everything.'

'Everything,' Jack echoed sarcastically. 'Sure, why not?'

She kissed him on the cheek and strolled serenely from

the room. Jack did a short pantomime of the anger he could not really bring himself to feel. He snorted, shook his head, pronouncedly untangled the phone cord. Then he sat heavily in his chair and picked up the receiver. The dial tone sounded like a reproach. He set it back down.

He stayed in his office for a few hours, reading weekly reports from his managers. Things were looking up. The economy was improving. More people needed care. Around eight, he heard the doorbell ring, followed by the dogs' barking and his wife's voice. Jack switched off the lamp but hesitated a moment in the darkness of his study. The day's bourbon and frustration had left his limbs numb and heavy. A swell of blood surged through his head, tunneling his vision with a liquid darkness. He waited for it to pass, his heart pounding in his ears and neck. Then, with a tremendous effort, he rose and walked into the hallway.

He was shocked by his son's appearance. In the two weeks since finishing school William had gained at least ten pounds – a puffy weight in his face and stomach. Faint streaks of red stretched across the flesh of his neck, wrists and elbows. His eyes seemed strangely unfocused.

They shook hands tentatively, the awkwardness compounded by the fact that both were left-handed yet shook with their right hands. Jack was accustomed to using the handshake in business situations, as a probe, a test of the other's will. William only shook hands with men who extended them, and then with an ironic indulgence. Jack found his son's hand stony, lifeless. He quickly let it go.

Two friends from the city had accompanied William. Both wore button-down shirts and had darkly limp hair pulled behind their ears. One – Dennis – was well over six feet tall and very thin, with a pockmarked face and bulging eyes that always seemed to be averted. The other – Chris – was much shorter and wore square-framed glasses that were tinted gray. Because the dogs rushed up and buried their noses in the strangers' crotches, Jack did not have to shake their hands.

He led the boys onto the screened porch and was surprised to find that it was already dark outside. He switched on a lamp, and almost immediately giant mosquitoes began to click against the screen. The young men arranged themselves in the chairs around a rectangular glass table. Jack made drinks at the cart and handed them out. There was a short silence after he sat.

'Billy, I want you to see something I've just bought,' he said, reaching below the chair and inserting a plug into the socket. He then nodded toward a purple ring that appeared on a tree some fifty feet from the porch.

'It's a bug zapper. That light is surrounded by a wire mesh that has electricity running through it. The bugs get fried in the wire as they rush the light. It uses a ten-pound collection bag. I have to change it every three days.'

William said something Jack did not catch.

'What?'

'Nothing.'

'Nothing?'

'Nothing.'

There was a long silence, during which they began to see flashes and hear the crack of the bug slaughter.

'They just keep coming,' Dennis said, transfixed.

'They never know what hits them,' Chris said.

Jack stole a glance at his son, who had gulped down his Scotch and was pouring himself another. Jack could tell by his expression that he knew he was being watched.

'So how are things going, Billy?'

'Things . . . ' William repeated, staring into his glass. He sat down and took a sip. 'Fine. Good. You know, all right.'

A dozen reproaches flashed in Jack's mind, but the presence of the two strangers kept him still. He turned to them.

'What is it you fellows do?'

There was a slight pause, as if they were translating the words.

'Well, we work in the same store as William,' Chris said.

'We play in a band, too,' Dennis said.

'Oh really? What sorts of things do you play?'

'All kinds of stuff. Pop, mostly.'

'Punk rock?' Jack asked, remembering the program he had seen that afternoon.

'Yeah, something like that.'

'You know, when I was your age, a punk was somebody who was always getting in trouble, somebody you avoided. Is that what this is all about?'

'It's about alienation,' William said.

'Aliens?'

'No. It's . . . never mind. You can't explain it.'

'I didn't think so.'

Jack stood and poured himself another drink. He asked the boys if they needed a refill, but they hadn't touched their glasses. William's was empty. Jack did not ask him.

'Hey, look at that,' Chris said.

Jack's two dogs, well-bred Afghans, had chased a raccoon into an ivy patch at the back of the yard. The raccoon had turned to make a stand, spitting and clawing with a surprising vigor. The dogs, teeth bared, pranced around the frightened animal as if they were in a show.

'Let 'em have their fun,' Jack said.

But the animal, after scratching one of the dogs below the eye, scrambled into a narrow drainage pipe. The dogs sniffed and whined for a while, then ran off in another direction.

'Dad, remember the kids with flippers?'

Jack looked at his son for a moment.

'Sure.'

'Tell these guys about them. They don't know about them.'

Jack told his son's friends about the children who had been damaged in the womb by some drug during the fifties and had been left with fleshy stumps for arms. He had worked at a non-profit center for them in the city for a while when William was young, devoting his evenings and weekends to balancing their books and overseeing personnel.

'He took me there one Saturday,' William said. 'I played with all these kids. They were building this huge fort with, uh, those wooden things – Lincoln Logs. They were so patient, really cool, but after a while I just freaked and hid in the boiler room. Those flippers, man.'

There was a pause. Jack moved his glass through tight circles, causing a small whirlpool of Scotch.

'What ever happened to that place?'

'It's still there.'

'Are those kids still there?'

'I don't know.'

There was a long silence, broken only by the settling of ice in glasses and crackling from the fluorescent machine in the back yard.

'This is really a nice house,' Chris said.

Jack looked around the porch, as if noticing it for the first time.

'We're thinking of moving somewhere a bit smaller now that the kids are moving out. Too many empty rooms.'

Jack saw his son looking at the cart.

'So what's your schedule look like for the next few months, Billy?'

'My schedule?'

'Your plans.'

'Oh, I'm gonna take it easy for a while, I guess. Maybe try to pick up a couple more shifts at the store so I can buy a new turntable.'

Before he could formulate a response, Jack saw a van from one of his homes approaching. He remembered having invited his mother to the dinner and immediately regretted it. He had counted on the presence of a crowd of relatives to occupy her. She lived in the finest of his homes, in a specially appointed room that he had taken personal charge of outfitting.

'Well, boys, would any of you care for dinner?'

'It's overwhelming,' Dennis said, gesturing to the food Mrs Allen had placed on the table.

'I was going to serve it buffet style, but with so few people . . . ' Her voice trailed off as she looked over the meal. There was a giant cauliflower – soft, steaming, covered with a crust of unevenly melted cheddar cheese and a sprinkling of breadcrumbs. There was a deep bowl of brown rice, laced with green onions and almonds. There were rolls, tanned on top, blackened on the bottom: there was a tossed salad, thickly garnished with walnuts. Two large bottles of California white wine stood on the counter, next to the built-in grill where Mrs Allen was putting the finishing touches to some steaks. Everyone stared as its blue flames danced beneath a rain of fat.

'That's an ingenious device,' Chris said.

'It certainly simplifies things,' Mrs Allen replied.

'Isn't there a smoke problem?'

'There's a fan underneath that draws the smoke down and away. Of course that kind of takes away the smoky taste, so I use this. Smell . . . '

She let them sniff from a small bottle of brown fluid.

'It's liquid smoke. You just pour a little bit on and it gets a hickory smell.'

Jack overlooked the table with a growing sense of satisfaction. The Scotch, the smell of food, his position at the head of the table all buoyed his spirits and caused him to forget his son's distant behavior. He sensed that he was regaining possession of the celebration. There was something almost musical in the scraping of plates and clinking of glasses.

'How's the violin coming along, Tommy?' Grandma Allen asked Dennis. She was a short, ugly woman who moved and spoke with an insular ferocity, as if she were somehow aware of her confusion, using it against the world.

There was an embarrassed silence as everyone continued to serve themselves.

'Fine,' Dennis said politely after a short while.

'Did you play that concert?'

'Yes Ma'am.'

'How the hell did it go?'

'They gave him a standing ovation,' Chris said proudly. 'They called him back for an encore. He played "The Flight of the Bumblebee" twice and still they would not let him go. The stage was littered with flowers. It was uncanny.'

The strangers had spoken without the slightest trace of sarcasm, yet there was something troubling to Jack about what they had done. He looked at his son for a while, but he was oblivious, immersed in wine and food.

The remainder of the meal went without incident, the only conversation being the polite chatter of Mrs Allen in response to the strangers' questions. Grandma Allen's delusions became vague enough to be ignored, although a couple of times she had to be quieted with a gentle touch on the wrist by her daughter-in-law. Jack continued to watch his son, who seemed to be totally self-absorbed. He drank down a half-dozen glasses of wine without seeming to taste them and ate a large portion of food with a bland greed. Occasionally, he said something to himself, but Jack could not distinguish the words.

They finished eating, the dishes were cleared. As his wife began to serve coffee, Jack excused himself and went into the study. The check and envelopes from the no-shows were lying on top of his desk. He gathered them and paused for a moment, combatting a swell of anguish. That feeling of a great task unfinished returned, forcing him to sit down. The evening was slipping from his hands. He had to do something to salvage it. He read over his check a few times, and this made him feel somewhat better. He headed back to the kitchen.

★

'Is everyone's glass full?'

The strangers had not touched their wine. William topped off his, then handed the bottle to his mother.

'I would like to propose a toast . . . Billy, there comes a time when . . . well, when we must . . . we are very proud of your achievement in earning a degree. We can all appreciate the amount of work and self-discipline it took to accomplish this. We hope it is the beginning of a long string of successes on your part. Here's to you, son.'

Glasses were raised, murmurs of agreement. Jack noticed that the strangers only wetted their lips with wine.

'Ann, will you pass these down to Billy?'

The first two envelopes contained cards from 'the dogs' and from William's sister. The others were from friends and relatives, including several small cash gifts amounting to sixty-five dollars. Last, he came to his parents' card. He opened it and slowly read the words Jack had written, as if they contained a great profundity. He then glanced at the check, smiled faintly and put it and the envelope on the pile, without comment.

'What do you have there, Billy?' Jack asked loudly.

'A very generous gift from my parents,' William said quietly, to no one in particular.

'Pass it around so everyone can see it.'

He smiled again and handed the check to Chris.

'You know,' William said, his voice still quiet and indirect, 'when I was very young, my father told me something that's stuck with me all these years. "You reap what you sow," he told me. "You reap what you sow."'

Jack felt a swell of emotion.

'That's not me, son. That's the good book.'

He surveyed the table. His wife was in tears. William continued to smile and avert his eyes. Even Grandma Allen seemed to be affected. But the instant he turned his gaze to the strangers, his growing sense of power turned into a feeling of utter helplessness. They were both staring at him with a brutal curiosity, as if he were some sort of specimen.

He tried at first to answer their gaze, but felt more and more transparent. He turned away.

'Ma, for Christ's sake, don't paw the thing like an animal! You'll get grease all over it,' he said to his mother, who was staring intently at the check. She looked around the table, blinking confusedly, as if trying to determine the origin of the voice. She then turned toward her son and spoke with a surprising lucidity.

'Don't you speak to me in that tone of voice, young man! Don't you call me an animal! How dare you? You son of a bitch! What would your father think if he were alive and could hear you speaking like that? Shame on you! How dare you!'

There was a long silence, during which the old woman seemed to recede into her vague world. Mrs Allen asked if anyone wanted tea and, before there was an answer, filled a kettle and put it on the stove. She told them that she had just bought the kettle at an import store. It was handmade in Germany, its spout especially designed to sound a D minor note as the water started to boil, then gradually ascend to D major as the steam pressure built. Just wait, she said, putting the burner on the highest level with a shaky hand.

The phone rang. William, who had gently taken the check from his grandmother, sprang up to answer. He spoke familiarly with the person on the other end, his voice lowering in concern.

'Chris, come here and talk to Andrew, man. You won't believe this.'

Chris took the phone from William, who disappeared into the living room. Chris listened intently, his face hardening. He hung up without a word and beckoned to Dennis, who joined him in a corner of the kitchen. They spoke in hushed tones, then slipped into the living room.

Jack drank down his wine, then refilled the glass from the half-empty bottle. He watched his wife collect dishes, his mother stare into uneaten vegetables. It was all he could do to lift his glass. The water finally boiled, hitting its perfect note. Mrs Allen switched it off, leaving the kettle on the stove. William walked back into the kitchen.

'We have to go.'

'Is something the matter?' Mrs Allen asked.

'Something's happened. We have to be on the scene tonight.'

'Go,' Jack said quietly.

His son nodded, never looking at his father.

He was awakened by a continuous crackling noise. His first thought was fire. He sat up quickly in bed, trying to isolate the noise. When he determined that it was in the yard, his muscles relaxed and he rubbed at the flesh at the bridge of his nose. He looked at his wife to see if she had been disturbed by his sudden movement, but she slept on. He walked over to the window.

What appeared to be a small bird had become involved in the bug-killing machine. The current caused it to shudder violently, as if still alive. Smoke was visible in the purple light. Below the machine, Jack saw what looked for an instant to be a statue. It was his mother. She was standing perfectly still, her skeletal body framed in the light that was shining through her thin gown. To either side of her were the dogs, also perfectly still. Jack stared at this sight until he felt himself falling asleep. He then put on his robe and went downstairs.

'It's a bat,' she explained as he walked up beside her. 'His echolocation must have gone on the fritz. He's history now, that's for damned sure.'

'Let's go inside,' Jack said.

After he put her to bed, he went to get the dogs. At first, they wouldn't obey his commands. They even resisted his tugs, keeping their gazes fixed on the smoking bat and emitting low growls. Jack had to beat them savagely before they would be led back to the house.

He returned to the yard, lit only by the still-running machine. Melted flesh had fused the animal to the wire grid. He had to pry it loose with a stick. Its wings had been burned off, leaving only a network of charred tendon. The small, hairless body looked like any other rodent. Jack had difficulty believing that it was ever capable of flight. Using two sticks, he levered it off the ground and chucked it into the ditch of an unfinished hedge.

He poured himself a cognac and went into the family room. He felt a strange impulse to hear some music, but found the selection of records unappealing. He opened the cabinet below the stereo. There were more albums, ones he had forgotten existed – records from the early years of his marriage, even some from before that. To one side was an untouched box of records – 'Great Operas'. His wife had won it at the club several years back. He tore at the cellophane and opened it, randomly selecting an album from the dozen inside.

He must have put it on in the middle of a piece, because the singing began almost immediately. The voices sounded like laughter. The music was lighter than air. Jack was soon asleep.

He awoke a short time later, troubled by a dream of cracking earth. He remained motionless for a while, his limbs heavy from awkward sleep. He felt an uneasiness about something in the room, but it took a while for him to figure out what it was. He realized he was hearing the same word, over and over, followed by the click of a stuck record.

'*Strazio . . . strazio . . . strazio . . . strazio . . .*'

He stood and gently lifted the needle from the record. Brand-new, he thought disgustedly. He filed the album back in the box and went to switch off the light and retrieve his glass. Beside the lamp was an ashtray his employees had given him as a gift in the early days. Jack stared into it for a moment, thinking it odd that it was dirty with ashes.

Nobody in the house smoked. Then he realized they were not cigarette ashes, but the residue of burnt paper. He picked up a charred sliver, making out a majority of his signature against the pale blue background. Above it, the first number of the sum he had so impulsively written in that morning. With abundant care, he set the slip of paper back in the ashtray, switched off the light and left the room.

Brilliant House

S hortly after the death of his daughter, Walter Smith
decided to rewire the house. There was really nothing
else to do. Walter had been forced to retire two months
before Paula died, so there wasn't anything left in the way
of work. And with Peg having gone the year before, there
was nothing stopping him from doing whatever he wanted.
In the days immediately after Paula's death he tried watching
television or going to strip bars or circling the Beltway in
his van, but soon realized that he was too old and tired to
develop bad habits. So he had a go at the circuitry.

What he had in mind was to centralize control of the
house's electrical system. It was something he'd always
wanted to do. He decided to wire everything to a control
board, which he would then place next to his and Peg's bed.
The work was hard, more strenuous than anything he had
undertaken since losing the leg. First he had to bypass the
basement fuse box, running a wire to carry the house's main
current upstairs. He then reconnected most of the
upstairs outlets and switches directly to his room. He took
pleasure in his work's crude efficiency, not bothering to
conceal the wires that ran through the house, leaving them

wrapped on the floor in loose waddings of insulation. Then he built the control board. He used aluminium and plywood, making it two foot by one foot. He installed both dimmers and switches. He then bolted it to the nightstand next to the bed. He had to move a lamp, a clock and Peg's pill tray to make room.

It took him two days' continuous work to complete the job. He went at it with the deliberate, compensatory patience of a partial man. After finishing he ate a big meal, removed the prosthetic and settled into bed with a pint of apricot brandy. He did a run-through, watching from his bed as shadows shifted in the hallway when he twisted the dimmer; listening to radios and the garbage disposal and the garage door spring into action, then stop dead, with each flick of the switch. He ran the board for a good hour before polishing off the bottle and falling into a dreamless sleep.

For three days, with the exception of trips to the bathroom or the stale-smelling refrigerator, he remained in bed. Nobody called. Nobody came to the door. Finally, Walter was getting the rest he felt due him. Thirty-six years pissed away building circuits for Anders. A leg lost in the Sicily campaign, a wife who left him with hardly a word. A year visiting Paula at Mercy, and now her gone. What the hell. He lay still for hours, listening to his pulse. Thirty-eight per minute. Four limb heart, three limb body.

He couldn't bring himself to blame Peg, really. She had borne the worst of it, visiting that thing they called Paula in hospital every day, speaking into her colorless ear and stroking her cold hand, seeing that the drip stayed clear, making sure that her bed sores didn't get too bad. That was what did it to her in the end – the sores. One day Walter came home from work and found her sitting perfectly still in front of the picture window in the living room, bags packed, tweed coat buttoned tight.

'It's those sores, Walt. I can't . . . '

Still, he wished she had been there at the end. The doctors at the hospital hadn't made any sense at first. They said that there was no electrical activity left in Paula's brain. It was news to Walter that there was electricity in the brain in the first place. Then they'd explained that meant she was brain dead, a less comforting but more comprehensible notion. He was asked if he would consent to a termination of life-support systems.

'You mean pull the plug?'

They just nodded and he said sure. Provided they could guarantee Paula was a no-hoper. The doctor said he couldn't do that, there was always a one in a million chance.

'We talking miracle here, doc?'

The man nodded. Walter thought of losing his leg on that land mine when nobody else even got a nosebleed. Of getting put out to pasture by Anders after all those years sweating over circuits. Of his wife's voice as she called a friend to take her away. He thought of those bed sores and the other kids walking away from that tangled car without a scratch. There was no use counting on miracles.

'Pull it, then,' Walter said. 'Just pull the damn thing right out of the wall.'

But even after Paula was gone, Walter couldn't stop thinking about what the doctor had said about that electricity in the brain.

He soon became bored with the new wiring, with his detached control of the house. So he thought it might be fun to randomize the whole thing. He made a run to a supplier in the city and brought in some additional tools from his van. He also bought a case of apricot brandy and a few magnums of that New York State pink champagne. He and Peg always had a sweet tooth for liquor.

There wasn't enough room on the dresser, so he cleared off the photos, vases and jewelry boxes to make room for the equipment. It didn't take long to rig the circuits so that a flip of a master switch would set the house buzzing, each light or appliance going like mad for a short time before giving way to another. Often more than one. He finished the job that night and opened a bottle of the pink champagne to celebrate. Then he hit the switch. It worked like a dream. Walter sat amid the random sound and light, laughing and swigging as his house went crazy.

He slept uneasily that night, awakened by occasional bursts from appliances or flashes of nearby light. A few times he was tempted to shut it all down but couldn't bring himself to turn off his handiwork. He slept on and off until late morning, dreaming fitfully of comets, fireworks, great forests ablaze. And there was that haunting thought, more of an image really – millions and millions of sparks of electricity flashing inside his head. It had been nagging at him for a month but during that night of random sound and light it came up in his mind and wouldn't go away. He woke for good to the sound of the doorbell, followed quickly by the realization that it was not attached to his board.

It was a young boy holding a clipboard. He announced that he was collecting sponsors for a balloon launch that was going on at some nearby church. Walter's head was pounding from sleeplessness and drink. It was as if he could almost hear the crackle of the currents in his brain. He was about to slam the door when there was a particularly raucous bit of electrical activity in the house. The boy's eyes lit up with curious delight.

'You like that?' Walter asked, his voice strangled by sweet, boozy phlegm.

'This is a neat house.'

He cleared his throat and had an idea.

'Come on in for a second. I'll sign up for your balloon.'

The boy stepped into the hallway.

'Somebody has my pen, though,' the boy said.

'Wait here and don't touch anything.'

Walter went into the kitchen and opened the desk drawer. On top of the tray of pens was a monkey wrench he'd stowed while working on his system. The low hum in his brain grew louder, coming in pulsing waves. He rubbed his forehead but it wouldn't go away. Just like the sound he'd heard for years when they'd cranked up a generator or a big oscilloscope at Anders Labs. But now it was on the inside. He picked up the tool and tested its density against the palm of his hand, then stuffed it in his back pocket and took a pen from the drawer.

The boy was laughing at the house's brilliance when he rejoined him. Walter signed his name and then reached back for the wrench. But just as his hand tightened on the cold metal there was a loud rattle from the kitchen as the blender flared on, accompanied by a pulse of light from the lamp near the door. The humming in his mind receded, as if bled by the house's surge. The boy laughed again and Walter let go of the wrench.

That night he heard children outside his house, gathering around various windows to see the crazy activity in the house. He was surprised that he didn't feel like driving them off. He lay still in his bed, sipping the sweet liquor that seemed to stay suspended in the top of his throat, straining to hear their laughter. The booze and laughter were good – they crowded the humming from his head. The children left after an hour or so. He passed another restless night.

The next day was spent bolstering the system, making it more powerful, more frenetic. Several of the bulbs surrounding Peg's makeup mirror blew. The motor in their ancient drier overheated, leaving a mist of acrid smoke through the house. Walter installed additional wiring and breakers that could handle more current. As he worked he thought about Paula.

There were four of them in the car, Paula and her friend Andrea and two boys from high school. Paula drove. They'd been drinking and smoking pot and driving around the subdivision when they'd decided to run a red light. A delivery van nailed them. The other three had walked away unhurt but not Paula. They'd used chainsaws and something called 'the jaws of life' to pull her free. Walter had been called to the scene by then – he remembered the sparks as the chainsaw cut into the car's metal. They fell around his daughter's strangely peaceful face. That was over a year ago. At first Walter had wanted Paula to wake up so he could ask her why she did something so stupid but gradually he just wanted her to wake up. And now they'd pulled the plug so he would never know.

Just after sunset, the children returned. He listened to them for a half-hour, then walked to the big window in the living room and tried beckoning them. They scattered. In the distance he could see a searchlight beat steadily across the sky, a pump of light that seemed to be in sync with the waves in his brain. He had an idea.

He went to the city the next morning for kliegs and spotlights. It took him two days to find the right equipment and set it up in the back yard. He put a spot on each corner of the house, facing the sky at an inward angle, so that their beams would cross a few hundred feet above the yard. He then studded the trees with the kliegs, positioning them to create four uniform rows of light lengthwise across the yard. Using the stepladder was difficult at first, but he soon reckoned a method of weight distribution and the work went smoothly. Although he had sought out the most powerful commercial equipment, the intensity of the outdoor lighting surprised him when he switched it on. He set up a chair and his box by the picture window so he could operate the lights individually, casting four neat strips of light across his yard.

The last thing he did was run a live wire to the large screen on the picture window. He had to be careful with this job – he laid off the brandy for a few hours before the delicate work. It was hard to stop drinking, especially now that the house was quiet. The electric hum in his brain had never been louder. When he finished he flipped the switch on the wire leading to the screen. He put his hand a few inches away from the mesh and felt the powerful vibrations. He turned on all the lights and opened a bottle of pink champagne.

The children appeared soon after, lingering at the edge of the brilliant yard. Walter cut off the outermost row and, after some hesitation, they crept forward to the light's new border. Walter let them settle in before he cut off the next row. Again they inched forward, a dozen shadows coming closer. He switched off the third row of lights and waited until they were all creeping forward before he relit the outermost row. The children stopped, trapped now between the walls of light. A few peeled off and fled through the hedge. But most remained in the strip of darkness. Walter then switched off the row nearest the house. He thought he could hear nervous laughter. His brain crackled so loud he could hardly think. The children crawled forward until they were faceless silhouettes just a few feet away from the window. Walter switched on the current to the screen, moving slowly so as not to frighten them. One of the children half stood, egged on by the rest. Walter's head and shoulders were shaking. The boy took a step forward, inching his face toward the screen.

One of the kliegs in the trees blew, showering sparks over the lawn. The cracking noise caused everyone to freeze. Walter's brain grew suddenly quiet, as if a switch had been thrown to stop the crackling. He wondered for an instant why that had happened just then, seconds before the child was about to touch the screen's electrified wires. Maybe it was his miracle. Walter turned off the current to the screen and moved forward slightly, showing himself in the light reflected from the yard.

'Scat,' he said.

The children ran, screaming and laughing, toward the sheltering darkness.

The Simulators

Theresa stood in the empty kitchen, trying to figure out what was going on.

'I'm thirsty,' her son repeated.

'The cups are all packed. They aren't here yet. You'll have to use the thermos top.'

'Where is it?'

'I don't know. On the floor somewhere. You'll have to look for it.'

Michael returned a few moments later with the thermos. He unscrewed the cup and held it under the faucet, which he jerked on with an angry motion. There was a loud sneezing noise, followed by a series of profound bangs from somewhere beneath the floor.

'There's no water.'

Theresa told her son to try the hot water. That, too, only produced a rapid cough.

'There's no water.'

Theresa stared at the faucet. Max was supposed to have taken care of this. She reached over the counter and flipped the switch for the light above the sink. Nothing. She flipped the disposal switch. Again, nothing. An empty jack showed there was no phone. First the movers don't show, and now this. Max was supposed to have taken care of it. That's why he'd come ahead and she'd been left to drive the kids. Why had he told her that 'everything was set' when he'd phoned the hotel the night before? And why did he . . .

'Mom, I have to go to the bathroom.'

Now it was Joy who stood in the doorway.

'All right, honey. Just go down the hall. It's the last door on the left.'

Her daughter's face contracted in thought.

'Do you know which one is left?'

Joy shook her head.

'OK, wave goodbye.'

Joy smiled and raised her right arm, closing her fingers several times into a small fist.

'Now, that's your right. The other is your left. All right?'

Joy nodded and ran down the hall. Theresa wondered if her husband had remembered at least to put paper in the bathrooms. Something occurred to her.

'Michael, quick go tell your sister not to go to the bathroom.'

'Gross . . . '

'Michael, please.'

Theresa stopped, recognizing that impenetrable look on her son's face. She walked quickly to the bathroom, finding Joy sitting in semidarkness, her left hand shoved between her bared thighs, her right thumb deep in her mouth. Before Theresa could speak she let out a short, grunting sigh. Her legs fell slightly apart, her face loosened and her thumb fell away from her mouth. She smiled proudly at her mother.

'Mom, why won't the toilet flush?'

'Because the water isn't on.'

'Why not?'

'Because your father forgot to tell the water man to come.'

'Does he have fish eyes?'

'Who?'

'Water man.'

'No, sweetheart, he's just a normal man whose job it is to turn on the water.'

Theresa had established camp in the family room, a spacious, sunken den with thick wall-to-wall carpeting and a blocked fireplace. The other rooms, with their bare floors and hollow echoes, were uninhabitable. With the grudging help of her son she'd emptied the car, piling their possessions in the middle of the room. They looked pitifully sparse. There were three suitcases, a shopping bag full of snacks, a couple of tattered blankets, Joy's stuffed animals. Theresa checked her watch. Almost one. She had to decide whether to wait for someone to show up or find a phone and make some calls. She thought of trying to reach Max, but remembered that he had said he would be busy that morning and would meet them that lunchtime at the house. She reasoned she had better wait. He would be furious if she . . .

There was a knock at the door. The children stared at Theresa, who stared back at them.

'Water man,' Joy whispered.

Theresa went to the front door. There was a young man in a brown jumpsuit holding a parcel under his arm.

'Are you here for the water?'

'No, thank you,' he answered. 'I was wondering if you could sign for this package. Your neighbors aren't home.'

'O yes, of course.' Theresa signed the clipboard beside his steady finger and took the package from him. It was so light that it could have been empty. She carried it back to the den and placed it among their possessions.

'Was that water man?'

'No, dear. It was the UP man.'

'Did he float above you?'

'What?'

'The up man.'

'No, he's just a normal man who delivers packages.'

Joy, looking dissatisfied, began to suck her thumb and

arrange her animals around the fireplace. Theresa decided to make a few calls. She had begun to give her son instructions before noticing that he was gone.

'Joy, where's your brother?'

'He went sploring.'

'I thought I told you to stay put.'

'I did.'

Theresa walked to the door and called out her son's name. There was a strange, hysterical quality to her voice as it echoed through the empty rooms. After several seconds, she heard a thump and then the sound of something being dragged along the floor. Michael soon appeared in the kitchen, pulling a large cardboard box behind him.

'What did you find, honey?'

'Nothing.'

He pulled the box into the den, tipping it over and spilling its contents onto the carpet. It was full of pieces from several different games. She recognized chessmen, dice, letter squares, wooden building blocks. The functions of the rest were difficult to determine. They were obviously the remnants of broken or incomplete games, left behind by the previous owners.

'Michael, that's just a bunch of junk. Don't mess with it.'

But he had already begun to sort it according to some inner logic. Joy watched him for a while, then began to help, instantly knowing her duties through the wordless understanding they sometimes shared. Theresa explained to them that she had to leave for a short while to make some phone calls, and that they should stay put. If they had to use the bathroom they should use the one that was already dirty. They nodded distantly and continued to organize the game pieces.

It took her a half-hour to find a pay phone whose receiver had not been torn off. She searched out her husband's card in her purse. There was no answer on his private line, so she called the receptionist. The phone rang twice, then was answered by a recording.

'You have reached Exact Simulations System Incorporated. Please hold the line – your call will be handled in order. This call is being taped.'

The tape continued.

'ESS is a bold new company on the cutting edge of simulation technology. A subsidiary of Anders Electronics, ESS specializes in the recreation of those environments which scientific man needs to master in his quest to understand and conquer nature. Whether it be a deep-sea tank or the command module of a space . . . '

'Hello, thank you for calling ESS.'

'Yes, I'm trying to reach Dr Max Venables.'

The receptionist's voice was grave.

'May I ask who's calling please?'

'This is his wife.'

'Perhaps you should speak with Dr Joiner, Mrs Venables.'

There was a soft click as she was put on hold. Theresa felt a wave of fear pass through her. She thought of hanging up. Through the receiver, she heard a voice that sounded as if it were speaking from behind a glass barrier. It seemed angry. She began to distinguish other distant-sounding voices. It was as if she were standing outside a crowded room. There was another click.

'Mrs Venables, this is Paul Joiner. Where are you?'

'I'm standing outside the 7-11 in Indian Hills. Is Max there?'

'Is he *here*?'

'At work.'

'Listen . . . Max . . . when did you last speak with him?'

'Last night. Why?'

'What did he tell you?'

'That everything was set.'

There was a pause. Theresa thought she heard her husband's boss sigh.

'Mrs Venables, I don't know what to say. Max hasn't reported for work yet. We were thinking maybe with the move and what not, but now . . . '

She realized that it was her turn to speak, but couldn't think of anything to say.

'Listen, when you guys work this out or whatever, have him call. There's a lot of stuff in the balance here.'

She nodded and replaced the receiver on its hook. She looked numbly into the shop, where children clustered around a video game, transfixed by its brilliant lights.

She was willing to follow certain lines of thought to their logical conclusions – that Max had been in some sort of accident which they were trying to keep secret from her, or perhaps this was some elaborate, sick joke. Other paths of thought she refused to follow. She looked up the number of the Department of Public Works and pushed a few more coins into the phone. After a dozen rings a surly-sounding woman answered.

'I want to know if you've been contacted about turning on the water at my house.'

'Have you contacted us?'

Theresa paused for a moment.

'I don't know.'

'Well I don't either.'

'How could I find out?'

'Is your water on?'

'No.'

'Then you haven't contacted us.'

'I'm trying to find out if my husband has been in touch with you.'

'Cat got his tongue?'

'No. I mean, I don't know where he is. So I figured that if I could see whether he'd been in touch with you I'd know . . . I'd know what? . . . I'd know more than I do now.'

There was a long silence. Again, Theresa began to hear distant voices from other conversations.

'Hello?'

'Listen lady, aren't there better ways of finding your husband than this?'

Theresa hung up the phone. She tried to think of who to call next. The other utilities would of course be no help, the movers were on the road somewhere. She closed her eyes and pictured her husband explaining everything, his small eyes and small hands moving in manic synchronicity. It's just that she couldn't imagine what he would be saying.

Theresa remembered something. It had seemed at the time like one of those many small things about Max she would never figure out. They'd been packing in preparation for the move, loading box after box with the accumulated possessions of twelve years together. They'd saved two months' worth of morning papers as insulation. Yet Max was strangely careless in wrapping their things, simply throwing a few sheets into the bottom of the box, placing in stacks of china and crystal, then throwing a few more sheets of paper on top. She couldn't understand it – he was always such a meticulous man. When she'd gently challenged him about it he'd angrily asked her who had the PhD, anyway. Theresa had waited until he'd gone out before unpacking the boxes and carefully wrapping the things in old newspaper.

And then she began to think about the vast, silent area of his personality she had once believed to be great intelligence, but gradually came to know as a frigid mass of prejudice, superstition and petty hatreds that . . .

The pay phone rang. She picked it up.

'Is Theresa there?' A child's voice.

'This is she.'

There was a long pause. It occurred to her that she hadn't given anyone this number.

'Theresa?'

'Yes.'

'You aren't Theresa.'

'Yes I am.'

'No you're not. Theresa is my friend. She's six. You talk old.'

'What number are you calling?'

'Theresa's.'

'Spell it out.'

The child recited the number. Theresa told her that she had misdialled. She hung up, wanting nothing more than to go home, yet decided to make one more call.

'Morgan Realty, how may I help you?'

'This is Theresa Venables. May I speak with Ms Castle?'

There was a pause, during which Theresa could hear a noise like a large book being dropped.

'Mrs Venables, hello, this is Amy Castle. I'm glad you called. We've been trying to reach you for two days. Now, what's this about a stop payment order being placed on your down payment check? If you wanted to arrange an alternative form of finance you should have contacted . . . '

Theresa hung up the phone and walked slowly to her station wagon.

The children weren't in the house when she returned. Theresa rushed from empty room to empty room, calling out their names. She looked everywhere, eventually returning to the family room, trying to collect her thoughts. She was missing a shoe. She searched the house again, finding it in the master bedroom. This calmed her somewhat. She walked to the still open front door and looked out at the quiet street.

Max had taken them. Everything was clear now. This had all been orchestrated so that he could get the kids. But the absurdity of this notion soon occurred to her. Why would he go to such lengths to get something he already had? He didn't seem to care for them that much, anyway.

The street was still, except for the clicks of squirrels in the trees and the sound of traffic on the Beltway. Everything was so perfect. Even the large piles of branches that lined the road every fifty feet or so were uniformly trim. Theresa looked at the neighboring houses and wondered what would happen if she knocked on the door with her story. She didn't dare.

The kids turned a corner and walked casually toward the house, Joy a little way in front of Michael. She seemed to be talking to herself. He was spitting every time he passed a branch pile. They saw Theresa but didn't increase their pace. When they reached the door, Joy simply said hello and Michael averted his face. Theresa squatted in front of him as he tried to pass and cupped his face with her large hands. His mouth was puffy, lined with dry blood. She gently forced it open and saw that one of his teeth was missing.

'What happened?'

'Nothing,' Michael said, jerking away from her. A shrill whistle now accompanied his voice and breathing, sharpening his pained and sarcastic tone. Theresa bolted the door and followed her children into the den, sitting with them among the game pieces.

'Michael, I want you to tell me where you went and how you lost your tooth.'

'I didn't lose it.'

She winced at the whistling sound.

'Mike, that's no answer, is it?'

He was saying nothing, fiddling with the pieces on the floor. Theresa noticed that they had been arranged into several distinct groups.

'What's for dinner?'

A fresh wave of despair swept through Theresa. She had forgotten to buy food after making the calls. She reached for the bag of crushed chips, cookies and warm drinks. The children watched her dubiously. She dreaded another trip out of the house.

'Let's play a game,' she said.

'We can't. Everything's missing,' Michael said.

'We have enough to make a game of our own.'

97

'What's it called?' Joy asked.

'Ad Hoc.' Theresa thought that was the right phrase. Anyway, it sounded like something you'd call a game.

'What are the rules?'

Some things he had done deliberately. Others he had simply left undone. They would have to leave this place.

'Well, let's say that you can use any piece you want. And we'll each take turns making up a rule as we go along. You have to try to make a better rule than the last person.'

'I don't understand,' Joy said.

'You will, honey. Michael, you go first.'

'The chess guys can capture any other piece.'

'Except the black marbles,' Joy said.

'Everybody gets one black marble,' Theresa added.

If he's coming, now would be the time he would arrive. Apologetic, sheepish, talking a mile a minute. But he wasn't going to come.

'The idea is to get rid of all the pieces,' Theresa said.

'That's silly,' Joy said.

'So's this game.' Michael scattered the few pieces they had managed to divide and stalked into the kitchen.

'What do we play now, Mom?'

Tell yourself. Either he's left you and taken everything or he's done something horrible and left it all a mess out of apathy or madness. She thought of that dark, silent realm in him. No, stop. What do we do now? Tell yourself. This house isn't yours, this town isn't yours, you'll have to give it all up. And now Michael's tooth. She should find a dentist.

Theresa collected a group of face cards her son had arranged on the floor, shuffled them and placed the pile on the carpet.

'Let's play Story People. What you do is pick one of these cards and then you make up a story about it.'

'What kind of story?'

'Well . . . '

'One that rhymes!' Joy said.

'All right. And you roll the dice to see how many rhymes you have to make. Go ahead, sweetheart.'

'Jack of hearts . . . three.'

They would be hungry later. There was nothing to sleep on. They would have to wash up. She knew she'd have to take them out of here by the end of the day, but wondered if she could find the courage simply to rise from the floor. It felt so good, not to move.

'The Jack of Hearts, had to start, but he made a fart,' Joy sang.

Theresa looked with shock at her daughter, who smiled back proudly.

'Michael told me that word,' she said.

Theresa hadn't the will or the energy to scold her. She drew a card from the deck. King of Diamonds. She rolled the dice. Four. She stared at the tattered card, unable to think.

'Go ahead, Mom. It's your turn.'

'I can't . . . '

'She's too dumb to think of a rhyme,' said Michael, who had been lurking in the doorway. 'It's my turn now.'

He ran up to them and grabbed the cards, flinging them in Theresa's face.

'You're stupid!' he screamed, his whistle piercing the house's emptiness.

'Michael!'

He danced away from her outstretched arms, staring at her with wild eyes.

'Who told you to say that?'

'You're stupid!'

'Michael, why are you saying this? What did he say to you? What do you know?'

'Stupid! Stupid! Stupid!'

'Michael, is your father dead?'

Her question startled them into silence. They remained perfectly still, the only noise being their excited breathing – Michael's sharp whistles, Theresa's asthmatic gulps. Joy had fled to the opposite end of the room. Theresa struggled to her feet. She didn't bother to repeat the question. She knew the look in her son's eyes. He wasn't talking.

She stumbled out of the room. The toilet reeked from an afternoon's use without flushing. She tried to put her head over it but couldn't endure the stench. So she pivoted on her stinging knees and vomited into the bathtub. She was careful to soil only the end near the drain, and thought this was a funny thing to do. After she finished, she rocked backwards against the wall. The tile was cool on her sweating flesh. She could hear the children at the other end of the house. They were swearing loudly, banging the walls, tearing things apart.

When she returned, the room seemed strangely peaceful, as if they had finally settled in. The children had ripped open the neighbor's parcel, spreading hundreds of worm-like styrofoam insulators over the carpet. The box had contained a small china vase which they'd smashed against the brick fireplace. Sharp, radiant fragments lay about the darkened opening like jewels spread outside a cave. Ripped pieces of paper and nut-sized game fragments crunched under Theresa's feet as she approached Joy, who slept among her torn animals. She covered her with a blanket, then sat near Michael, who had found a few crayons and was drawing on the walls. There were bloody faces, burning trees, stick figures firing cannons, a sinking ship. He was making faint explosive sounds with every slash of color. The whistling from the gap in his teeth gave the sound a frightening, inhuman quality. Theresa watched him work for a while.

'How's your tooth?'

Michael reached into his pocket and pulled the bloody, long-rooted tooth from it. Theresa took it from him, looked at it, then handed it back.

'Does it hurt?'

'It's OK.' He continued the battle.

'Some mess,' Theresa said softly, looking around the room.

'Do we have to clean it up?'

'No. We'll leave it for the next people.'

'Do we have to leave?'

'Not yet.'

Theresa slept for a while next to her daughter, dreaming that someone handed her a phone and told her she'd better hurry. She said hello and a man's voice told her to hang up immediately. 'No hesitation!' She looked for the hook but there was none. The man began to yell and told her that she had better hang up the fucking phone or he'd break her fat neck. She held it as far away from her body as possible but the man's voice only became louder.

She woke up and walked to the bathroom. She wished that there was some way she could rinse her acidic, desiccated mouth. The smell was powerful but she soon grew accustomed to it. She slowly removed her clothes and hung them on the shower bar. Her own body's odors wafted momentarily stronger than the toilet's. She removed a tampon from her purse and changed, neatly folding the used one in wrapping and placing it behind the cistern. She removed a few moistened towels from their foil and began to clean her skin. The cleanser stung momentarily. She began with her neck. When she reached her ankles she heard a rustling noise behind her. She turned quickly but saw nothing, though she thought she heard retreating footsteps. She dressed and returned to the den, listening at the door.

'Mommy has a tail,' she heard Joy say.

'Gross.'

'It's white.'

There was a pause.

'Maybe she's a water man.'

'Maybe,' Michael answered.

★

The car's exhaust fumes came out heavy and slow in the dusk chill. After loading their few possessions, Theresa and Michael watched a truck as it made halting progress down the street, stopping in front of the branch piles. A group of men in white suits swarmed from it at each pause and fed the wood into a small trailer, which exploded with an instant of sound and then resumed its persistent hum. Theresa went back into the house to get her daughter. Though still asleep, she began to speak softly as her mother carried her from the house.

'It's a cartoon. It snows but it isn't cold. And then the snow melts and it turns into . . . water man! He doesn't have a body but can pour himself into anything, boxes and cups, even other people's bodies. He goes into you and out of you and into somebody else. And then . . . then . . . '

Theresa laid her gently among the pillows and suitcases at the back of the car. The truck had reached the other end of the street, its explosions distant now. Theresa dropped into the driver's seat, put the car in reverse and looked over at her son. He was staring straight ahead, his eyes dark and active, his shrill breath sounding periodic shrieks. Theresa reached out to stroke his hair but couldn't complete the motion.

'Drive fast as hell, Mom,' he said.

The Iron Man

Wendell Hoyt imagined he could trace the random flight of voices up into the great cavity of the cooling tower. He pictured the young engineers' words mixing into one distant, melancholy sound above. It careened from emptiness to emptiness, finally resonating with something deep in his memory – another voice echoing between concrete and empty space. He tried in vain to connect the voice with a face, but it remained abstract, disembodied. His mind raced through numerous images, but he could not isolate the speaker or the place.

Hoyt and the engineers were discussing how to best bury the incomplete nuclear power plant. Cost overruns, failed inspections, the defeat of a bond referendum and a drop in energy demand had combined to cause the utility to halt construction at the halfway point. The piping was intact, as were the ancillary buildings and one tower. Hoyt, who had been promoted to manage the plant, was now given the job of disposing of the equipment with a minimum of financial loss.

'Bottom line, gentlemen,' Hoyt said.

'Well, first of all, scrap this goddamned tower and sell

the materials to the dago contractors in the city. They love to wash their cash in garbage like this.'

'Yeah, but keep the piping intact. You're bound to find a buyer for that if the price is right.'

'Japan. Korea.'

'The PRC.'

'The Arabs would love to get ahold of this sucker.'

'They should be so lucky.'

Hoyt remembered. The first day of May, 1939. He had cut school, or maybe there was a teachers' strike. He toured the Stroh's brewery for the free pretzels and beer, then used his lunch money to buy a cheap seat at Briggs Stadium, upper deck, down the right field foul line. Even though the Yankees were in town, he was relatively alone in those outer reaches.

Gehrig's first two at-bats were easy outs – an infield fly and a grounder to short. Hoyt had watched the first baseman's every move, from the way he stretched with the bat behind his shoulders to his casual manner of warming up the infielders – one two-hopper to their left, one to their right. They seemed to be throwing the ball back to him easily.

His third at-bat was against a young relief pitcher. Wiseguy kid, a giant killer who threw nothing but high heat. The first three pitches were up around the eyes, as if mocking the batter. The next pitch was chest high, but Gehrig was late on it, popping up a weak foul.

The ball sailed over Hoyt's head, landing some twenty seats away from him. It bounced up ten rows, then ricocheted back down to his level. His only competition was two skinny kids with Tiger caps, but they went with the first bounce and put themselves out of the race. Hoyt easily beat them to the ball, which was slowly rolling down the steps. He held it high. The two kids smiled enviously at him. Hoyt then looked down to the field, still holding the ball aloft. The batter was bent over, applying rosin to the bat handle.

The next pitch was high and tight – base on balls. The

next day, Gehrig told Joe McCarthy to take him out of the line-up. He missed his first game in 2,130, never played again. Two months later, Hoyt heard that echoing voice over the radio. Within two years, Gehrig was dead.

Now, Hoyt looked at the young engineers, whose echoes had long since faded away. He pulled his executive blue hardhat down on his head with a jaunty, athletic motion.

'Thank you, gentlemen. Type up those recommendations and submit them to my secretary.'

Wendell stared at the large frying pan, deftly turning the vegetables through the hot oil. Occasionally, he would sip from the cup of rum-laced decaffeinated coffee on the counter. He tried to clear his mind, imagining that the pungent steam condensing on his face and the muted fluorescent light could somehow clean away the day's troubles.

His wife, still foggy from her pre-dinner nap, walked slowly into the room. Wendell smiled gently at her, his eyes darting instinctively over the depression in her chest. He went to the refrigerator and got the paper cup full of vitamins with the day's date on it. Elizabeth laughed ironically when he handed it to her.

'I must have the most expensive urine in the world,' she said.

'Come on now.'

'Just joking,' she said in a silly voice.

'Attitude is half of it.'

'I know.'

He moved the vegetables.

'I got a new client today,' she said. 'The other one, Douglas, the homosexual, well, he quit the program. The new man is really interesting. Ben. He's rather pathetic but also sort of dignified. He's unemployed. His wife works at a school cafeteria. He's very fat – he must weigh three hundred pounds. They've been treating him for depression and compulsive eating. He was so funny – he kept asking my permission to do little things. Light a cigarette, eat a mint. You know. I explained to him that we were supposed to be peers but I think he likes to be told. We made good progress. Talked about his unemployment and decided it was making him into a passive type. I couldn't help but feel it was strange because he's so big and strong.'

'What did he do?'

'Oh. Well.' Wendell turned towards her. 'He was a welder. You know, at the power station.'

They watched each other silently for a moment, Elizabeth shrugging her shoulders. Wendell turned off the burner and served her special dinner.

Wendell made a chopping motion with his right hand into his left wrist, then leaned forward slightly and chopped at the back of his right knee with the same hand. Facing him twenty yards away was a younger man screaming insults. Wendell pointed at him, then raised his finger to his lips in a stern, fatherly gesture. The man quieted.

Wendell retrieved his yellow flag and jogged into the midst of the defensive backfield. Normally, he would have ejected the coach, but the game was close. It was the last of the season, for the championship of the local Youth League. The penalty made it third and long – passing situation. Yet the offense ran a perfect draw play to the tailback, trapping the nose guard and left tackle and suckering the linebackers outside by sending the other two backs into the flats. The tailback was into the secondary almost immediately, absorbing a hit by the safety on a limp leg, then spinning free. Wendell froze, letting the action pass him by, then wheeled and pursued the back, his whistle wriggling across his chest like a captive animal.

The boy was fast, but Wendell's longer stride allowed him to stay a constant five yards behind the runner. Nobody was going to catch him, but the back was still running hard. Wendell found himself transfixed by the beauty of the boy's stride, the perfect athletic grace of his motion. He imagined that he and the runner were frozen in some timeless field, that they were destined to run like this forever. But the boy eventually slowed up, dropped the ball and curved through the endzone in a wide arc. Wendell put the whistle in his mouth and raised his hands above his head. The boy stopped and put his hands on his knees. He was soon mobbed by his teammates.

Wendell retrieved the ball and placed it on the two and a half yard line. The players began to settle into their respective huddles. Wendell took a pad from his back pocket and made some marks on it. He felt a tap on his shoulder. The young coach, smiling self-consciously, shrugged his shoulders and nodded.

They had tickets for the community theater that night, but Elizabeth was too exhausted to go out. She went to bed after dinner. Wendell caught up on some paperwork, then fixed himself a drink and turned on a ballgame. He dozed for a while, waking with a sudden thought. He went into the front hallway and pulled down the folding steps that led up to the attic.

He was surprised that the light still worked. A quarter-inch patina of dust coated the boxes, exposed pipes and haphazard pieces of sheet metal that cluttered the attic. Wendell had to brush it away to read the labels on the boxes: 'Taxes', 'Christmas Ornaments', 'Photos', 'Warranties'. He smiled. His wife was a saver. He located the box marked 'Misc.' and tore it open. He pushed aside trophies, pen holders, ugly but expensive gifts, a case of mint edition coins from Europe – but he could not find Gehrig's ball. Wendell sat back against a beam. It had most likely been lost in one of the innumerable shuffles of their life together. He sat in the stillness for a while until the dust began to affect his breathing. He switched off the light and went to bed.

Dr P. G. Gokhale, an official of the Energy Ministry of the Indian government, was cooking Elizabeth's vegetables tonight. After taking the executive on an exhaustive tour of the plant that day, Wendell had invited him home for dinner. It was Gokhale's first visit to the U S, and Wendell figured he was experiencing enough that was traumatic without eating at a hotel restaurant.

It had been a tiring session for both men. Gokhale, an engineer by training, had been tough and exacting in his questions. He had scrupulously ignored the young engineers' confident rhetoric and jokes, attending only to Hoyt. The tone of the entire episode had been coldly respectful – Hoyt's quiet persistence matching Gokhale's polite skepticism. Wendell was frustrated not only by Gokhale's reticence, but also by his inability to make nonverbal connections with the foreigner. The grammar of the Indian's gestures was so different - the gentle, ironic twist of his upper lip, his way of blinking instead of nodding yes, the barely perceptible rocking of his torso as he listened to explanations. What he was thinking, what he was feeling, was perfectly masked, and Wendell could not figure how to get past that veneer. After several failed jokes and confidences, Hoyt had resorted to a dry, patronizing monotone that seemed to die echoless in the empty space of the power plant.

The two men warmed up slightly to one another on the commute home, meeting, as if by truce, on a neutral ground of politeness. Their conversation remained impersonal, yet they were able to make slight jokes about their cultures and governments. It soon became apparent that their professional lives were similar – early technical training, ten-year careers in the armed forces, management jobs in later life. Both men shared an ironic view of their industry and the younger engineers who now dominated it.

Elizabeth had spent a long time preparing herself for their first guest in months. Wendell was shocked – he could hardly detect her ill health beneath the carefully applied makeup and energetic gestures. Gokhale seemed instantly charmed by her, abandoning his choppy, efficient diction for a smooth and gracious speech. Wendell realized that he was perfectly fluent in English and that his lapses in comprehension at the plant had been a strategy for gaining additional information.

As Elizabeth took Gokhale for a tour of the house, Wendell quickly began to prepare her macrobiotic dinner. They hadn't discussed it, but Wendell noticed that there were only two servings of the stuffed chicken Elizabeth was cooking. By the time she and Gokhale had returned, he had her dinner going. Elizabeth made two Scotches for the men. Gokhale watched Wendell cooking for a moment.

'Ah, I notice you are cooking a vegetarian meal. This is a good thing, because I neglected to tell you when you extended your invitation that I am a devout vegetarian. It is something I began while in college in England. Kidney pies!' He made a face.

Wendell and his wife looked at one another. He shook his head slightly, she nodded and went to get additional food. Wendell surreptitiously switched off the oven. Without a word being spoken, as if by mutual agreement, Gokhale took the spatula from Hoyt and began to stir the vegetables.

'Would you by chance have cumin? Turmeric? Coriander? The red pepper?'

Elizabeth accommodated him the best she could, digging deep into her spice cabinet. Gokhale turned the heat up to the next-to-highest level, expertly turning the food through the now red liquid. A pungent steam curved through the fluorescent stove light, inhaled by the fan above. Noticing that occasional drops of the hot liquid were splattering Gokhale's vest and tie, Elizabeth helped him into an apron that said 'I'm the Cook' across the front.

He asked for cucumber and yoghurt and whipped up a cool paste which he explained would be necessary to assuage the heat of the main course. Gokhale's grimly polite demeanor was completely transformed by now. He spoke of his love of cooking, of the markets in Delhi where peppers were piled in mounds as high as a house, of playing hide and seek with English children in a field of poppies when he was a boy.

The meal was like nothing the Hoyts had tasted before. The vegetables possessed a soft, enduring warmth that seemed to radiate through their bodies. When the spice would become too much, the cool yoghurt would balance its fire. Wendell noticed that his wife ate with a vigorous appetite he had not seen since before the cancer had been diagnosed.

Just as they were finishing, Wendell remembered something one of the young engineers had given him. A cassette. 'It's Gokhale's wife,' he had explained. 'A guy from our subsidiary in Delhi sent it over. Apparently, this dude's wife is some kind of popular religious singer or something. I listened to it – it's crap. Eee-yuh-yuh-yuh. You know, Third World shit. But put it on if you want to soften him up. They're supposed to be pretty close.'

Wendell walked into the den off the kitchen and put it into the tape deck. As it was rewinding, he studied the cassette box. On the front was a picture of Mrs Gokhale. She was handsome and dignified, possessing the same shy smile as her husband. Around the photo were dozens of crudely sketched flowers. Wendell could not read the writing.

The music came on just as he retook his seat. Gokhale stopped eating and stared for a moment into his steaming dish. He then carefully placed his fork beside the plate and looked up at Hoyt, nodding. Elizabeth watched the two men curiously.

'It is my wife,' Gokhale explained.

Her voice was unaccompanied. It sounded at first like a chant – a monotonous, almost inhuman sound to the Hoyts. Soon, however, different rhythms began to assert themselves. They could detect a barely controlled anguish, a profound loneliness that seemed to drive the voice in search of a proper tenor. Yet, again and again, it would return to a single, plaintive, diminishing note that ended with a sudden sigh of breath.

Gokhale sat perfectly still, only his eyes registering the music. It was as if he were hearing it for the first time. Wendell felt a swell of anxiety at the deep effect the music was having on the man, but soon was transfixed by it. They sat silently through the entire side of the tape, until the voice ended and there was a rush of electronic noise, followed by the machine switching itself off.

'That was very beautiful,' Elizabeth said.

'Yes, it was, I think,' Gokhale replied. 'She's dead, you know.'

Wendell awoke in the middle of the night, realizing that his wife was not in bed. The bathroom door was open, the light off. He listened to the house but could hear only the usual noises.

He found her in the kitchen, slicing the chicken breasts they had left in the oven. Mrs Gokhale's voice filtered in softly from the den.

'I'll make sandwiches later.'

Wendell poured himself a cup of cold coffee and placed it in the microwave. Elizabeth wrapped the chicken in tinfoil, waiting until the buzzer sounded before she spoke.

'I guess I'll be going into Mercy tomorrow and getting back on the chemo program.'

Wendell held the cup to his mouth but did not drink, preferring instead the steam that soaked his face and penetrated his sinuses.

'I'm afraid, Hoyt. This way requires too much of me. I'm afraid I'm not strong enough. What if I can't endure? What if I'm too weak? I want something else to have to be strong.'

'You are strong, Elizabeth.'

'Lots of people are, you know. And they don't make it.'

Wendell reached across the table and took her hand in

his. She hated her large, veined hands. He used to tell her they had character.

'All right.'

Gokhale would make his proposal over a lunch meeting, then Hoyt would return home and take Elizabeth to Mercy. He knew Gokhale's proposal would be low and wondered how they would go about the difficult negotiations after the previous night. Business as usual, he thought. They'd wear their masks.

Unable to get back to sleep, he had gone to the plant, arriving before any of his crew. He chatted with the security guard for a while and learned that once again kids had been drinking and dancing in the tower late at night.

'They say they like the acoustics,' he explained. 'They have those big radio boxes. They were very polite, actually. Offered me a beer. They didn't break anything or do any graffiti, so I just escorted them out.'

Wendell nodded and walked from the shed. He thought of the previous guard, a tense young veteran who had pulled his gun on three Oriental boys who were riding their minibikes in the tower. When Wendell had confronted him about it later, the man had touched the leather strap of his holster, saying he had a job to do. He had nodded rhythmically the entire time he spoke, his hard eyes averted. Wendell had to let him go. He always seemed to be letting people go, letting things go.

Instead of entering on the ground level, he ascended a spiral staircase to a platform high inside the building. The predawn darkness was broken only by a naked bulb he switched on. The light dissipated after twenty feet or so, suggesting the void. He reckoned the platform must be over one hundred and fifty feet above the tower's concrete floor.

He recalled the weekend's game, remembered running in stride with the back. He closed his eyes and again imagined he was in that timeless field, moving with such speed and grace that it was almost identical to being perfectly still.

He put his hands on the railing and leaned forward. His heart sped with vertigo.

'Today.'

Instead of echoing in some pattern around the darkness, his voice, after a momentary silence, reverberated from every direction. He leaned back and repeated the word, but the echo from above was slight, inconsequential.

He noticed a crate of elbow joints and large bolts in a corner of the platform. He picked up a fist-sized bolt, bounced it a few times in his hand as if weighing it, then deftly threw a hard fastball into the darkness. It banged off the opposing wall, then clamored along the floor of the tower, the original sounds becoming mixed with the echoes. The next pitch – a two-pound elbow joint – was a big, lazy curve that didn't even make the opposing wall. This was followed by a slider, more heat, sidearm curves, even a knuckler with a lug wrench. He was pitching the objects so rapidly that soon the tower was a din of falling metal.

Even after the last pitch had settled on the floor, Wendell still thought he could hear residual noise, like murmuring voices. He draped his windbreaker over the railing and removed his hardhat, holding it to his side. He looked down.

'Today,' he said.

'Today,' the tower said back.

'I consider myself.'

'I consider myself.'

'The luckiest man.'

'The luckiest man.'

'On the face of the earth . . . '

Chlorine

'Because they don't think it's right for people to use it after what happened. Because they hate the thought of it. Because they're stupid . . . That's his window, the one with the light. Could you imagine having people splashing and yelling and everything with him up there listening? I mean, sure, *he'd* understand, but *they* wouldn't. So they drained it. I remember when they did it – beginning of August. It was weird. Dad ran a hose out to the curb and then sucked on it until the water began to flow. It shot out real strong and he got some in his lungs. He didn't gag or anything but had this real bad cough for a couple of days. From the chemicals. Anyway, David was brought home that afternoon and we had to carry him around back to fit the bed through the sliding glass doors. He saw the empty pool but didn't say anything . . . He used to be able to do three and a half laps underwater.'

'Can't he hear us now?'

'I guess.'

'Won't your folks be mad?'

'No. Their consciences are clear.'

'What do you mean?'

They passed the tequila silently. They were sitting in the deep end, beneath the diving board. A portable radio played softly between them, its sounds echoing erratically around the tiles.

'So what happened?'

She paused, smiling slightly.

'The bats – you should've seen this – these bats used to swoop down and skim the surface and then take off again. So quick. It was unbelievable. Now sometimes they come down, all the way down to the bottom. They'll skim the concrete, get all confused and panic and career all over the place. Their echo thing gets screwed up.'

'You've seen this?'

'David has.'

He took the bottle from her and screwed the top on so hard that he almost stripped it.

'So what happened?'

She closed her eyes and made guttural noises of differing volumes and pitch, testing their reverberations. He tapped the bottle on the tile, then stood and walked to the shallow end, turned, squatted, let the bottle roll down the slope. It went slowly at first, sped up radically when it went down the depression in the pool's middle, then evened its momentum. She caught it before it reached the far wall, unscrewed the top and took a sip. He walked back to her, zigzagging, his back exaggeratedly stiff. He stood above her.

'Have you ever seen one of those underwater windows, where you can look into a pool from the outside?'

She said nothing.

'I always used to wonder what'd happen if you broke one of them.'

'The water would come sloshing out and flood the entire world.'

'I mean to the swimmers.'

'They'd feel naked. Cheated.'

'Are we underwater?' he asked.

She said nothing.

'I'm getting drunk.'

'Me too.'

He held his hand above his head, moving it until its shadow crossed her face.

'So what happened?' she asked in a mocking, basso voice.

He sat next to her and took her left hand softly between both of his. She pulled it away petulantly, but immediately put it back.

'Twenty-five years to the day after their wedding my parents had a twenty-fifth wedding anniversary.'

'Here?'

'Yeah. It was a big deal. People jetted in from all over. Catered food, balloons, people in bathing suits, people in tuxedos.'

'Swimming?'

'Some. Not much at first. It started out real sedate. There was champagne in those plastic long-stemmed glasses. Piano music on the stereo. Chinese lanterns. David was really funny. He was wearing a three-piece suit except that the third piece was these huge psychedelic swim trunks. He had a big cigar which he used to burst some of the balloons. That got it going. Someone was dunked in the pool. You know how these things go.'

'Yeah.'

'My grandmother got drunk and started to swear. My uncle tried to feel me up. My parents wouldn't stop dancing with each other. Gag gifts, incoherent toasts. My cousin Andrew sulking around, acting like this is the stupidest form of human behavior imaginable.'

'And you?'

'I loved it. I mean, it was like the whole thing had developed a personality, and so you could do anything you wanted and if it was stupid you could blame it on that personality.'

'So what happened?'

He felt a vague tremor in her hand.

'Everybody in the pool. Even those without bathing suits.

The men just rolled up their pants. Some women stripped down to their underwear. Nobody cared. We started to do jump-dive off the board.'

'What's that?'

'Well, you run to the end of the diving board, and just before you take off somebody'll scream "jump" or "dive", and you have to do what they say. Only there were dozens of people yelling, most saying things like dump or jive or banana, so it rapidly degenerated into a bellyflop contest. My dad, el blubber, was the best. His stomach was pink as anything but he was too tanked to give a shit.'

Another tremor.

'So David appears on the fucking roof. Like Zeus or something. Everybody shuts up. My mother starts to tell him to get down but somebody interrupts her and calls out "jump!" Like it's a big joke. Then some genius yells "dive!" and people catch on. David spreads his arms dramatically and people begin to clap and cheer. Yelling, screaming. Nobody believing he'll really do it but everybody secretly wishing he would. He puts his arms down and backs off, so things get a little quieter and we figure that's that. A few still yell. But he'd merely backed up to get a running start. All of a sudden he's over us, suspended, beginning to fall. Gasp, silence. It becomes apparent that maybe this isn't such a good idea. But my dad, still caught up in it all, yells out one final command. Jump! Not too loud, but he was the only one. It sort of hangs there next to David and drops with him. So there's my brother, airborne and scared, and my dad – belly pink, hair slicked back, eyes stupid with drink – yelling after it was too late to decide. As if David still could choose.'

There was a long silence.

'Well, he had a bit too much topspin. He begins to lean forward, like a ski jumper. Everybody's just frozen, watching, a few holding out their hands. Of course it takes him three hours to hit the pool. His head coming forward, inch by inch. He overshoots it. His feet catch the water all right, but his chin hooks the far edge. His head snapped back so hard I remember thinking, Wow. My brother David's head has just fallen off!

'So there we all are, gathered around the pool, looking down at my brother lying on the bottom. It looked like he was shivering but that was only the ripples in the water. A few people make to go get him but my uncle says "You're not supposed to move people with neck injuries." A long pause. Suddenly there's a splash and another wavy figure at the bottom. My cousin Andrew, all eighty-seven pounds of him, trying to fetch David. Then I'm in, swimming, touching his silent flesh. I remember thinking somebody'd pushed me in, but I guess it was just instinct. We maneuver him to the shallow end, then up to the surface. At this point, Dad and all the other men begin barking and bustling. Taking charge. Hysterics, ambulance, pots of coffee, good-looking interns rationally talking odds, Mom chewing on knotted Kleenex, me with my soggy underwear. Rock and roll.'

She stood up.

'That's what happened.'

'So they drain the pool.'

'Well what are you supposed to do when you feel like you've fucked up and allowed an awful thing to happen? You do something stupid and inappropriate and then you still feel bad but at least you're still in charge. It's not so strange.'

She pinched at the bridge of her nose. 'Anyway. I gotta pee.'

Although a late summer chill had cooled the night considerably, the air conditioning in the house was running. She thought that walking through the sliding glass doors was like opening a refrigerator. Her mother, abandoning a characteristic frugality, had kept the system going continually since David had been brought home. She said he was more comfortable this way.

Gripping each elbow close to her stomach, she walked quickly through the silent house. In the cool and dark, it seemed perfectly still, as if uninhabited for a long time. She stopped at the slightly open door to the family room. Her parents, backs to her, were watching a silent TV. The screen was blank, except for a network logo and the words: Video Difficulty. PLEASE STAND BY. The channel switcher dangled loosely in her father's left hand.

'Mom?'

She didn't move.

'Dad?'

He didn't move.

'Mom?'

'Yes?' she answered, without moving.

'Do you want me to bathe him?'

'No dear, I'll do it.'

'I put the sponge near his sink.'

She didn't reply.

He sat in the deep end for a short while, watching a distant spotlight move through the sky, wondering if any bats would be swooping in. He looked up at the sole lighted window, his mind a blank. He stood and scrambled out of the pool. He looked at the sliding doors for a moment, then walked to the far end of the yard, ducking behind a shed and unzipping his pants. He stood amid a collection of life preservers, long rakes, plastic balls, a basketball hoop with floats attached to it. He urinated on an overturned white bucket, the steam rising through a beam of light from the house. When he finished he kicked the bucket over. A strong chemical odor brought tears to his eyes and made him cough a few times. He looked more closely at the yellow oval of grass that had been covered by the bucket. A pattern of bones lay neatly within it, as if the remnants of some ritual. He could now discern the remains of some mammal, surrounded by a half-dozen small replicas, its litter, their claws and skulls pointing towards the larger skeleton's underbelly. They seemed to glow with an aura of chemical white, picked clean by fumes.

He heard her calling his name, her voice echoing from the bottom of the pool. Using his foot, he moved the bucket to its original position, then rejoined her.

Cherokee

Not long after he figured out that his wife was cheating on him, Lloyd Carrier bought a short-wave radio. It was something he'd been wanting to do for over a year, what with the kids off at college and June now working. He'd been spending a lot of time on his own and he didn't particularly like it. A radio would be a good way to occupy his thoughts. Get out of himself, get things off his chest. And now that he was convinced that his wife was unfaithful, there was nothing stopping him.

Lloyd hadn't worked a radio for thirty years, not since his hitch in the Army Signal Corps during the Korean War. Yet as he rigged up the unit in the basement rec room he was surprised how readily it all came back to him. The true/false test on the FCC license application was a piece of cake. It didn't take long for him to get the transceiver working – in two days he was able to eavesdrop on the airwaves, listening to the voices drifting in and out of the radio's shrill, constant noise. He was surprised how distant some of the callers were – Oklahoma City, St Kitts, a place called Anglesey. A few times he was tempted to respond to distant beckons, but prudence got the best of him. The FCC application had made it clear that severe penalties awaited unlicensed broadcasts. He could only listen for now. So he sat glued to the radio until three am, when June would be arriving home.

She'd taken the job as a paramedic soon after Bill and Wendy had left for college. Seventeen months separated the children but Bill had been kept back a year because of dyslexia. So they left home together. Knowing it would create a big empty in the house, June had taken refresher courses in nursing so she could start as an ambulance paramedic for the local fire department the moment they left. She worked the night shift, 6 pm to 2.30 am.

Lloyd made it clear to anybody who asked that he didn't have a problem with June working. Having watched other men bristle as their wives attempted to occupy themselves after the kids had grown up, he'd told himself that he wasn't going to stand in her way. She had been a nurse before they married and Lloyd knew she had never been altogether happy with giving it up. He didn't even mind the hours she worked – he liked learning how to cook, it was something he'd always wanted to do.

The problem, of course, was June's affair with her partner. Karl was in his late thirties, a heavyset man with a droopy moustache and expressionless brown eyes. He'd been a medic in Nam but was one of those vets who seemed to have come through it without much trouble. He'd tried to become a doctor after returning but his entrance exam scores were too low. So he worked as an ambulance driver. Lloyd had met him a few times and had thought him to be a steady, unexceptional sort of guy.

Which is probably why it took him so long to figure out what was happening. That, and the fact that June was fifteen years older than Karl. Despite the unlikeliness of the whole thing, however, he was sure they were lovers. It wasn't as if he had clear proof like photographs or a teary confession or an anonymous eyewitness account. In fact, when he first began to suspect June's infidelity, he'd thought of getting such proof by following them, but had quickly realized the impossibility of trailing a speeding ambulance through quiet suburban streets.

But there was enough evidence for Lloyd's mind. First, there was the fact that some nights June would come home different, a thrilled, irrational light in her eyes. Then there was her habit of drifting off, abandoning conversations, even when it was she who was speaking. And there was her increased sexual appetite, which seemed contradictory to Lloyd until he'd leafed through a magazine at the dentist's and seen it listed as one of the Ten Sure Signs of Adultery. It made sense when he thought about it, really. The most conclusive bit of evidence, the clincher, was the cowboy boots.

She'd worn them home from work a few months after taking the job. Lloyd had noticed them right off but hadn't said anything, waiting for her to explain. They were expensive-looking, light green, decorated with intricate swirls. Lloyd had sat in the kitchen while she'd fixed herself a late dinner, listening to the sharp sound they made on the tile. Yet she'd said nothing until he'd complimented her on them the following morning.

'Karl gave them to me.'

'Generous of him.'

'I'd said I'd always wanted a pair and so he just went out and bought them. I don't know how he knew my size but they fit like a dream.'

She was looking at them as she spoke, clicking them together like Dorothy in *The Wizard of Oz*. From that moment he knew there was something going on.

Lloyd stayed in the basement until she came home, listening to the sound of the boots on the kitchen floor above him. He closed down the radio and went up to her. She was eating microwaved eggs, staring out the window at the searchlight that had been cutting through the local sky all week. Woolgathering. Thinking of Karl.

'You eat?' she asked after finally noticing him.

'Yes.'

He sat opposite her.

'Busy night?'

'I was just thinking about that. You must be a mind-reader.'

Lloyd waited.

'Not too bad, except for this old guy we had to pick up at Anders Gardens. Some kids broke his jaw. Just for no reason, it seems. Could have killed him. Kids.'

Lloyd let enough time pass to make it seem that he'd thought about what she had said.

'Say, what are those boots of yours made out of, anyway?' he asked as casually as he could.

'Eel skin.' She didn't seem surprised by the question.

Lloyd sat with her a while longer, then went up to get some sleep before work.

He passed the next few nights listening to his radio, turning the dial slowly through several frequencies, moving sometimes beyond the short-wave zones prescribed to hacks. He captured all sorts of traffic, from local AM stations to broadcasts originating as far away as California and Canada. Every once in a while he'd catch a voice speaking in a language he didn't understand. It was then that he would think of the Cherokees.

That was back in Korea, during the war. He'd been working for nearly a year as a regimental radio operator just north of Seoul. The work was pretty routine – lots of supply requisitions, personnel and death notices, stuff like that. Most of the guys in his unit were bored with the work and wanted to get into cryptography or combat units. But not Lloyd. He'd heard enough about frostbite and dysentery and stray mortar rounds to prefer the centrally heated office and three squares a day on offer at HQ.

But then a truckload of operators had been wiped out by a land mine and he was transferred to a frontline unit. It was a miserable three months. The none-too-distant thud of mortars, the endless bug-outs, the astonishing cold of the Korean winter. And the dogs, everywhere you looked, mangy and scavenging dogs. He never actually saw battle, although a few times sniper fire caused him to take cover. The work soon settled into a sort of manic routine – he was one of the radiomen linking combat troops to senior officers at command posts. Sometimes he was the bearer of horrific news, yet even then he never felt anything more than remotely endangered.

The only really remarkable thing about the job was the Cherokees. He was never sure how many there were in all but there were always a few hanging around the Quonset radio hut. They were attached to deep reconnaissance platoons – one of them would accompany these daring units as they probed, often behind enemy lines, broadcasting back information to a fellow Indian in his native tongue to avoid detection. The Chicom intelligence officers who intercepted this traffic, with their English educations and rigorous study of the vagaries of Brooklynese, must have been puzzled to distraction. It was probably the only truly ingenious thing Lloyd ever saw the Army do.

He'd tried to make friends with the Cherokees but didn't get too far – they were proud people who did their jobs well and kept to themselves. He once asked the least imposing of them to teach him a few words but the man had said that you had to be Cherokee to learn the language. He'd said it in a matter-of-fact, slightly melancholy way that caused Lloyd no offense. So he'd settled for eavesdropping on their talk, which he found much more beautiful than the shrill, rapid Chinese and Korean which regularly came across the airwaves. Deep and terse and steady, full of long vowels and impenetrable consonants. Once or twice he convinced himself he'd picked up a few words or even a phrase, but had long since forgotten what they might have been.

As he twisted through the frequencies on the fourth night of operating his radio, Lloyd became entangled in the band reserved for the emergency services. The voices sounded much closer and clearer than any others he had heard. They were hard to understand at first, with their numbers and codes and catch phrases. But the longer he listened the more he thought he understood.

Then he heard June. Just for a moment, responding to a request for her position. 'Come back to me' was what she said, followed by an explanation that they were returning to the station, that the call had been a hoax. Lloyd was surprised at the confidence of her voice, its depth and assuredness as she rattled off lingo he had never heard her use. He listened to the emergency band for another hour but didn't hear her again.

Her confident voice made Lloyd think back to the time she had practised CPR on him, just after she'd started the refresher course. He was a reluctant dummy but there was no getting out of it. She made him strip off his shirt and lie on his back on the living-room floor. He tried to joke with her at first but she was all business. She started by pumping his chest, too hard at first, briefly knocking the wind from him. But then she got into the rhythm and was soon in sync with his heart's beat. He could feel the blood rushing to his head, to his extremities.

'Lloyd!'

'Sorry, it's just . . . '

She waited for him to 'settle down' before practising the kiss of life. The sensation of having air forced into his lungs was unpleasant at first, as was her pincer grip on his nose and the angle of his head. Yet he soon became giddy and began to enjoy it. He again grew aroused and wanted to make love to her, but just before moving caught a glimpse of her eyes – clinical, cold, as if he really were on the verge of death, some sort of victim. He lay still until she finished.

He made her a special dinner on that fourth night of the radio. Chicken Kiev. He had a hard time stuffing the breasts with garlic sauce – he was glad he'd bought a half-dozen of them. He would use the mangled ones to make stew later.

She was two hours late. Someone had called in sick and she'd had to stay on duty until they found a replacement. Lloyd saw that look in her eyes the moment she walked in the door. Sated, distracted. He served her the meal but she didn't seem to notice it was special, even when she cut into the chicken and the buttery juice spurted out.

'Busy night, then?'

'We had one bad call. Right before getting off. Some old woman had stroked out on the back lawn of her son's house. The funny thing was it was right beneath this bug catcher thing, you know one of those with the purple light, so as we worked her we had to listen to this crackling noise as it fried the bugs. Her son told us there had been a bat caught in it earlier, said the old lady had been staring at the light all night.'

'She die?'

'O yeah.'

When he got home the next evening there was a note saying she'd been called into work early and might be very late. There'd been a major emergency. Yeah sure, he thought.

After a quick dinner he tuned his radio to the emergency frequencies, thinking of Karl's droopy moustache, of his wife's hot breath in his lungs the night she practised CPR, of those boots. After a few minutes he realized that she hadn't been lying about one small thing – there was something big happening on the Beltway. It came in puzzle pieces of excited language. Multiple shooting. Sniper. Officer down. Exit 11. Come back to me.

Then, once again, he heard her. She was reporting their location, saying they'd arrived at the scene but no further assistance was necessary. He could hear Karl's drone in the background as he spoke with someone else, probably a cop filling him in on what was going on. June soon gave way to other, more urgent voices. Lloyd was tempted to use his transmitter to call out to her, but he couldn't think of anything to say. He soon found himself thinking about the Cherokees again.

He'd been working alone that night – the rest of the radiomen had gone to watch *My Darling Clementine* in the canteen. There had been a lull in the fighting, so when the broadcast first came in it had taken Lloyd a moment to react. It was a recon unit nobody was expecting to hear from until the next day. He'd acknowledged his call letters, then grabbed the pencil to take down the message. A voice had replied in Cherokee. He'd responded that the message had not been copied, that they had to come back to him. So it had been repeated in the language he couldn't understand. He'd realized what was happening. They were in trouble and needed help but couldn't give their position in English for fear of detection. He'd raced to the movie tent, finding a small group of Cherokees seated at the back, engrossed in the film. Yet by the time they had returned the radio had gone silent. The platoon was listed as missing the next day. He was shipped home a month later and never did find out what had happened to them.

The next night Lloyd bought a bottle of Old Crow and tuned his radio to the local emergency frequencies. He'd thought of what to say. It took him almost an hour, and a good part of the bottle, to work up the nerve to speak. Starting softly, fueling his voice with regular swigs, he began to say: 'I know. I know what you're doing. I know.' It was almost a chant, the way he repeated it. He stopped every now and then, listening for her voice. When it didn't come he would continue, just like the first time. Three sentences, the middle one the longest.

Just before midnight he finally heard her. Requesting a break. There, he thought. A break – I'll bet. Finally. Caught you.

A few minutes later he heard the click of her boots on the kitchen floor above him. He stayed where he was, confused, wondering for an instant if she had brought Karl to the house. She appeared in the door a few seconds later. The transmitter hummed.

'What the hell is it you think you're doing, Lloyd?' she asked softly, staring at the radio, as if noticing it for the first time. 'I heard your voice.'

He looked away.

'You know what I'm doing,' he said softly. 'You know what I mean.'

'No, I don't. But I do know you could get in a lot of trouble for using those frequencies. You could go to jail. I've convinced Karl not to report who you are even though everybody is really angry about it and dying to find out.'

'That's big of him,' Lloyd said.

She took a step into the room.

'What is with you, Lloyd? Are you crazy? What is all this "I know" nonsense?'

He looked at her.

'About you and Karl. I know.'

He knew from the look on her face that he was wrong, even as he said it.

'What? What? You big fool. What are you talking about? Karl, he could almost be our son. Me and Karl, how on earth did you come to think such . . . '

'Well what about the boots?' Lloyd asked desperately.

'The boots? The *boots*? Is that what this is all about?'

He didn't answer.

'Jesus H. Christ. I'll tell you about these boots, even though you don't deserve an explanation. Karl bought me these after I saved somebody's life. All right? There was a car crash and some girl was trapped and we couldn't pull her free. And Karl couldn't squeeze in and so I had to give her first aid. Even as the firemen were cutting her loose. It was the hardest thing I've ever done. And when I was in there with all these sparks flying around Karl said, you know to keep my mind off it, Karl started asking me if there was one thing in the world I could have that I didn't have, what would it be? I guess this was a trick he learned over in Viet Nam. You know, keep the mind occupied. So I thought and thought but all I could come up with was a pair of eel-skin boots. And so he bought them for me. But only because we're friends and because he was proud. He knew how hard it was and he . . . was proud.'

'Why didn't you ever tell me this?'

'Because you never asked.'

'I ask.'

'You say "Busy night?" and I know damn well it means you don't really want to know.'

There was a silence.

'There's other things, though,' Lloyd said weakly.

'Such as?'

'Such as the look in your eyes when you come home. Such as the way you drift off some times.' He looked at the radio, as if for help. 'And your appetites.'

'All right, yes, I admit I've changed a bit from working this job.' Her anger was subsiding. 'But not like you think. It has nothing to do with Karl or anything like that. It's the work itself. It's going out night after night and seeing these people who are sick or hurting or even dead. It's looking into their eyes. It's . . . '

'Helping them?'

'No, Lloyd.'

She wasn't angry at all now, but distant. Just like Lloyd had been saying.

'You forget those ones right away, the ones you can help. It's the other ones. Like that girl trapped in the car or that old woman who'd stroked out the other night. I can't stop thinking about them. They make me feel so . . . alive. More alive than I've ever felt.'

She said nothing more. The only sound left in the room was the crackle of the radio, the echo of voices around the subdivision.